Midnight Waltz

by

Barbarba Stephens

Odyssey Books Inc., Silver Spring, MD

Published by
Odyssey Books, Inc.
9501 Monroe Street
Silver Spring, MD 20910

ISBN: 1-878634-02-X

Published in the United States of America

February 1991

Dedication

For my goddaughter, Heidi Noele Jones.

Chapter One

Twenty-six year old Sylvia Random made her way out of the crowded baggage area of the Dallas airport, amid turning heads and admiring glances. Her six-foot willowy body, elegantly clad in an emerald green silk suit and matching high-heeled leather sandals, moved with free-swaying motions through the automatic glass doors into the early August evening. Absently, she tucked her shoulder-length dark brown hair behind her ears, displaying a copper-colored oval face with high cheekbones. She stood for a moment, allowing her large brown eyes to search the curb, and instinctively threw up a hand to hail a taxi.

"The Bennington Hotel," she instructed the driver in a husky, breathy voice as she slipped into the passenger seat. The young man placed her luggage in the trunk of the cab before pulling into the rush hour traffic.

Sylvia allowed herself to relax for the first time during her busy day as she closed her eyes and settled herself for the twenty-minute ride into the city.

As he drove, the young driver shifted his eyes between the expressway and the rear-view mirror, where he had a good view of Sylvia. "You a model?" he asked, causing her to lift her heavily-lashed lids to meet his gaze in the mirror.

"No," she said, resuming her relaxed posture.

"A dancer?" he guessed again.

Sylvia smiled patiently at the young man, realizing she would have to give up her notion of relaxing. "I'm a buyer for Emary Oaks in Houston," she answered.

"Oooh, Emary Oaks. Ain't that that high-class art store? I heard of that place. I didn't know they hired beauty queens for buyers."

"You're very kind," Sylvia said, this time deliberately avoiding the young man's eyes.

"What do you buy?"

"Items for the Nook of International Treasures".

"International. Do you travel overseas a lot?"

"Yes."

"That sounds like an interesting job. But if anybody had asked *me*, I would've sworn you were a high-fashion model or a show business superstar."

"No," Sylvia said, her lips curling gently. "I'm just a buyer from Houston."

The cab pulled in front of the Bennington Hotel and Sylvia got out. Again heads turned as she swung into the hotel lobby. This time Sylvia acknowledged an admiring male glance with a smile.

"Hello, Miss Random," the desk clerk spoke to her cheerfully as he pushed the register in front of her for her signature. "Welcome back to Dallas. Business or pleasure?" he inquired, inspecting her approvingly.

"It's business this time, Raymond," she responded. "It's time to shop for Christmas."

"Oh, so that means we'll see a lot of you in the next few weeks. It's always a pleasure to have you with us,

Miss Random."

"Thank you, Raymond." She followed the bellman up to her room and, once inside, began unpacking her bags. Sylvia always traveled to Dallas with clothes that would be appropriate for a variety of occasions, since she had friends in Dallas who often invited her out to sample its exciting social life during her buying trips. As she unpacked, she decided she would try to plan something for the evening, since she hadn't scheduled any social activity.

She hung her clothes in the closet, then picked up the booklet highlighting the city's attractions from the dresser and began thumbing through the nightlife section. She noticed a concert featuring one of her favorite song stylists was in town, and promptly dialed the desk to ask Raymond if he could obtain a ticket for her. An hour later, Raymond called back to report the concert was sold out for the evening, but he had managed to obtain a ticket for the following night's performance. After trying several other sources with no success, she gave up. She would just have to settle for going to the concert the following night.

Actually, a quiet evening was what she needed, she resolved, making her way into the bathroom. She filled the tub with hot water, added some bath oil, and climbed in for a long, soothing soak. As she gently washed her skin, Sylvia mentally planned her activities for the following day. She would go shopping in the morning, have lunch with Paul, and later she would attend the concert. She loved music and looked forward to the concert. Her parents had taught her to appreciate all kinds of music, so she felt as much at home at a symphony concert featuring music by Brahms as she did at a gospel concert. As her mind wondered, she remembered a conversation she had with her father many years before. He had compared her to great music, and said she would often find herself an object of high regard because of her inherent charm and striking beauty. She must be aware of how fortunate she was, and accept the inevitable attention and adulation with grace and humility, he had advised. Sylvia smiled to herself. Her father was a romantic, and they adored each other. She respected his wisdom, and had always wisely taken his advice.

After her bath, Sylvia slipped into a soft cotton lilac dress and matching high-heeled sandals, and went to the hotel restaurant for dinner. She had just completed her meal of broiled trout and vegetable salad when the waiter brought a bottle of wine to her table. "Compliments of the gentleman at the table to your left," he said. "He'd like to join you for an after-dinner drink."

Sylvia shook her head slowly. "No thank you, and please return the wine to the gentleman."

"Madam, I was instructed to tell you if you chose not to accept the gentleman's offer," the waiter replied, "that he would like you to keep the wine with his sincere wish that your evening will be as lovely as you are beautiful."

Sylvia glanced over her shoulder at the stranger sitting at the next table and allowed her eyes to briefly meet his. He nodded. Smiling coolly, she turned back to the waiter. "Thank the gentleman for me," she said, as she picked up the wine and rose to leave. She left the restaurant and headed for her room, where she dressed for bed and read until she fell asleep.

The next morning Sylvia rose early, had breakfast and began her work day on North Stemmons Freeway in the Dallas Market Center Complex. She enjoyed this aspect of her job and always looked forward to shopping the markets. Having to buy items that appealed to those who had everything was quite a challenge. She delighted in her ability to excite the interests of the Emary Oaks customers. The shop had won national, as well as international, acclaim for its unique, and sometimes extravagant, items since Sylvia had become a buyer at the Nook of International Treasures. It had been earmarked as *the* shop to explore by tourists and natives alike.

For the Christmas season, Sylvia had decided to highlight items native to Texas. But now she had set as her goal the task of buying typical Emary Oaks objects for three or four of their basic customer types. She found several pieces of West German handcrafted lead crystal that she felt would appeal to practical shoppers. Soft sculptures of clowns and dancers from France, and African masks and wood carvings, were bought for art lovers. For those with simple, but elegant, tastes she purchased a couple of brass and hand-decorated porcelain lamps with pleated linen shades and three handcrafted mahogany vases. The customers with extravagant tastes—and the finances to support them—would be offered Chinese scrolls, and animals handcrafted in China which were made of solid silver and decorated with jade, coral, turquoise and mother of pearl. She added Swedish crystal to her basic stock, a bronze wine cooler, a couple of silver ice buckets, a hand-blown glass icer and several small antique vases from Spain. Most of the basic stock for the shop had been bought earlier in the year for the holidays, so she didn't feel pressured to buy hurriedly or in bulk.

By noon Sylvia had completed her shopping and left the Dallas Market Center Complex satisfied with her purchases. She hadn't found any native Texas items that she liked, but she had already planned two more shopping trips to Dallas during the next month. She was sure she would find something in time for Christmas. Now she had to hurry back to the hotel if she was to keep her date with Paul.

Paul Wright had befriended Sylvia four years ago when she first began buying for Emary Oaks. An expert Oriental art dealer, he had taken her under his wing and was instrumental in helping her develop skill in buying Oriental art. Over the years their friendship had grown and they often shared time together when Sylvia was in Dallas. She had arranged to meet Paul for a late lunch.

As soon as Sylvia had showered and changed, the phone rang. It was Paul announcing he was waiting in the lobby. Sylvia put the finishing touches on her makeup and hurried downstairs to meet him. It was always a pleasure to see Paul. A tall, elegant man in his late fifties, he reminded her of a fairer version of Cary Grant. He had a boyish charm, and his dark blond hair, with only a few flecks of gray, belied his years.

"Our usual place?" Paul asked, as they walked to the parking area together.

"That's fine," Sylvia replied. "I'm always in the mood to eat at L'Entrecote."

By the time their lunch of crab-rice salad served on

pineapple halves, buttered broccoli, hot French bread and iced tea arrived, Sylvia had filled Paul in on her shopping trip.

"I've decided to spotlight native Texas arts and crafts for holiday gift ideas," she explained as they ate their meal. "Do you know where I can find some unusual items for our customers?"

Paul thought for a moment. "As a matter of fact, I do have some ideas. There's a blacksmith in east Texas who makes unique ornamental objects such as fireplace tools and candelabras that you might find interesting. I think it would be worth a trip to see if he has any items that would fit the Emary Oaks image." Teasingly, he gave her a sidelong glance. "He's single and a very handsome young man, too," he added. Paul had often tried to play matchmaker for Sylvia and some of his young friends, but his efforts had always met with abysmal failure.

"Paul, will you ever stop?" Sylvia smiled broadly as she jotted the information down on her note pad.

"No. It appears that once I begin a project, no matter what it is, I can't put it aside until it has been either successfully launched or completed. Presently," he said, mocking a frown and sighing deeply, "I'm hooked on my `match Sylvia with a fine young man' campaign and I'm determined to see it through."

Their eyes locked for a moment in friendly battle before Sylvia lowered her lashes and Paul continued to speak. "There's a young artist with a studio here just east of downtown who is simply magnificent. I personally feel his Texas landscapes and seascapes, and his paintings depicting everyday life in the big cities and small towns of Texas, would appeal to most art lovers.

I've bought several of his works for myself and so have many of my friends."

"He *must* be magnificent," Sylvia said, growing excited at the prospect of getting started on her new project right away. "Maybe I'll stop by there on my way back to the hotel. What's his address?"

"I'm going very near his studio as soon as we leave here. I'll drive you there."

After lunch, they drove along the busy freeway in the late afternoon heat. "I miss not having my car this trip," Sylvia remarked. "I had to leave it in the shop for repairs."

"Aha, the splendid white-on-white '38 Cadillac V-16 Club Coupe. It's a beauty, Sylvia."

"I enjoy driving it."

"Well, since you're without transportation ...," Paul began.

"Oooh nooo," Sylvia interrupted, laughing heartily.

"Certainly you haven't made plans for the evening."

"Yes, I have," she informed him smugly.

"I've been invited to a party tonight and this artist whose work I'm taking you to see will be there." Paul spoke as if he hadn't detected the note of protest in Sylvia's voice. "Come with me, I think you'll like him." His deep blue eyes were serious as he quickly glanced at Sylvia.

"Paul," she pleaded, "no more fix-ups with your friends. It won't work."

"This one is different, Sylvia." His broad smile wrinkled his deeply-tanned face.

"They all are, Paul," she told him. "I love you for caring about me, but I'm just not in the mood for a party tonight *or* to meet some man who'll have to stand on a chair in order to look me in the eyes." They both laughed.

"This man won't have to," Paul informed her as he stopped in front of the studio and quickly walked around the car to help her out. "He's extremely talented, handsome, much taller than you, and very eligible."

"Terrific," Sylvia said. "If he's lucky enough to be in the studio when I go in, I'll ask for his hand in marriage."

"Not a bad idea," Paul laughed. Taking her fingers in his, he added, "I won't go in with you because I have some other appointments, but tell whomever is there that you're a friend of mine and you'll receive the royal treatment." He kissed her cheek lightly.

"Thank you, Paul."

"What will you do tonight?" he asked, as he walked back around to the driver's side of the car.

"Oh, I'm attending a concert."

"Alone?"

"Yes, alone."

"Are you sure I can't persuade you to accompany me tonight?"

"Positive."

"All right," he conceded. "I have some more ideas for your special Christmas project, but I need to do a little research on them first. I'll call you next week. Enjoy the concert."

"I will," she said, "and thanks again."

Although she tried to deny it to herself, Sylvia entered

the small studio hoping to see the young artist Paul had so attractively described. Instead she was greeted by an elegant woman in her mid-forties.

"Hello," the woman's soft voice came from across a huge desk in the corner. "Would you like some assistance or do you prefer to look around?"

"I'd like to browse on my own," Sylvia said.

"Of course," the woman responded, "but please don't hesitate to ask if you have any questions."

"Thank you."

Sylvia began her browsing with several oil paintings hanging on a side wall that conveyed great skill and versatility in style, and moved around the room with deliberation, becoming increasingly absorbed in the works. Her searching eyes found exciting and powerful pen and ink drawings and water colors of romantic views of nature. She realized she was viewing the work of a remarkable artist, and happily began choosing canvases appropriate for the Nook of International Treasures. She chose seven pen and ink drawings depicting scenes of rural life in Texas and three water colors of landscapes and placed them on the large, intricately-carved wooden desk.

"Are these all for you?" the woman asked hesitantly.

"No," Sylvia said, reexamining one of the pen and ink drawings. "I'd like to make arrangements to sell the two oil paintings on the left front wall and these canvases," she spread her hands over the desk, "in a shop in Emary Oaks Specialty Store in Houston called the Nook of International Treasures. And the small oil painting of the field of wild flowers hanging by the window, I'd like to purchase for myself." She turned to look at the woman who was looking at her with surprise.

"Emary Oaks?" she asked, and slowly her long graceful fingers touched her throat.

"Yes," Sylvia said. Her forehead furrowed. "Do you know the store?"

"Of course," the woman answered. "Everyone knows Emary Oaks."

"I'm Sylvia Random," Sylvia said extending her hand, "the buyer for the Nook of International Treasures."

"It's a pleasure to meet you," the woman responded, taking her hand. "I'm Athena DeForest." Slowly, as if she anticipated someone stopping her, Athena took a pen and paper from the desk drawer and began writing out the transaction.

"I see the artist signs his work J. Udall," Sylvia observed. "What does the J. stand for?"

"Justin," Athena answered as she continued to write. "It's wonderful," she added, pausing to look at Sylvia, "that you've chosen some of his work to sell in your store. The exposure to that clientele will be wonderful for him."

Sylvia smiled warmly. "He's obviously a superb artist. It will be wonderful for our clientele to be exposed to Justin Udall."

Athena, surprised by the young woman's frank reply, watched her as she casually resumed her searching of the small room. "How did you find this studio?" she asked. "Did someone tell you about Justin?"

"Yes. As a matter of fact, one of his friends, Paul Wright, told me about him today. He's a big Justin Udall fan."

"Oh, Paul is a very dear friend of ours," Athena said. "I'm grateful he told you about Justin."

"I'm the fortunate one," Sylvia said, walking back to the desk and taking the chair across from Athena. "What can you tell me about the artist? I'd like some background information for our customers."

"Oh, more than you'd care to know. He's my brother." She laughed softly. "I have some brochures which describe Justin's work and training that you can give to your customers. I'll pack some of them with your shipment."

"That'll be perfect." Once more Sylvia allowed her large, inquisitive eyes to roam around the room. "How nice it must be to have such a talented relative," she said. "Are you an artist also?"

"No. I'm a retired nurse," Athena answered. "When Justin decided to open his work room to the public four months ago, I agreed to manage it for him. I love his work and I enjoy the atmosphere of the studio, but I have no artistic talents or aspirations."

They completed the transaction, allowing Sylvia to purchase the pen and ink drawings and take the oil paintings and water colors on consignment.

"You should receive these by the middle of next week," Athena told her.

Sylvia rose from her chair. "Fine," she said, starting towards the door.

"Wait," Athena called. "Have a glass of iced tea before you go back out in the heat."

"I'd love to," Sylvia replied after a moment's hesitation. She crossed the room and slipped back into the chair.

Athena served the tea and they chatted for almost an hour. They talked mostly about themselves and their careers before the conversation shifted to Justin's work, which they discussed briefly. During their short visit, a warm affection developed between the two women. They both knew when Sylvia rose to leave the second time that they had become friends.

"I'm having a dinner party tonight and Justin will be there," Athena said. "Please come. I'd like him to meet you."

"I've already made plans for the evening. I'm attending a concert."

"Then drop by after the concert is over," Athena insisted. "After buying so many pieces of Justin's work, you should at least know what he looks like."

"Yes, I think I would like to meet him," Sylvia said, surprising herself with her quick response. Athena gave her the address and she left the studio feeling a bit fickle.

Back in her hotel room, Sylvia showered and touched up her finger and toe nails which she always kept painted bright red. She thought about taking a short nap, but decided she wouldn't have time. Instead, she ordered a light dinner and ate in her room. Then she dressed and left for the concert.

For the next two hours, Sylvia was delightfully entertained by the melodic tones of Anita Baker. The concert was excellent, and she was glad she had attended. When the program was over, she made her way out of the crowded concert hall and took a taxi to Athena's home. She wondered, as she rode, what Paul would say when he saw her. She smiled to herself, realizing that indirectly he had won their little battle.

The taxi pulled into a long, circular driveway and stopped in front of a charming French colonial house nestled in a grove of tall Texas pines. Sylvia paid the driver, went to the door and rang the bell. The housekeeper, a plump attractive woman, greeted her and showed her to the living room where the other guests were gathered. The huge room was filled with formally-dressed people, who were scattered about the room in small clusters. Laughter and conversation wafted throughout the room.

Sylvia walked almost to the center of the room, before pausing to search out either Athena or Paul. She was stunning in a plum-colored silk chiffon strapless gown. The tight bodice revealed the firm swell of her full breasts. The skirt, which clung softly to her slender hips, was slit up the left side completely exposing one long shapely leg. A long, matching scarf hung casually over her right shoulder. Her high-heeled silk sandals were the exact color of her gown, and her red-tipped fingers clutched a rose petit point bag. Her hair had been combed back and tucked behind her ears, exposing her only jewelry—a pair of diamond stud earrings. Momentarily, the room fell silent as all eyes were gradually drawn to her.

"I'm so glad you were able to come," Athena said, rushing over to her. "How was the concert?"

"Lovely."

They moved across the room, as Athena introduced her to several guests. Finally they approached a group and Sylvia knew immediately she was at last face to face with Justin Udall.

"This is Sylvia Ransom, the young woman I told you about earlier," Athena told her brother. "She bought the thirteen works this afternoon."

"Thirteen is an unlucky number," an attractive, petite woman, who was clutching Justin's arm possessively, commented.

Sylvia turned her head quickly, flashed a warm and charming smile at the woman, and replied in her huskiest and breathiest voice, "Only if one has a superstitious mentality."

"And Sylvia, this is Polly Vance," Athena hastily completed the intoductions.

Justin, with great aplomb, took Sylvia's hand in both of his and smiled down at her dispassionately. "It's good to meet the young woman who made such a favorable impression on my sister," he said. "Athena has said very complimentary things about you."

"Your sister is very kind," Sylvia replied, enjoying the fact that she had to look up to make eye contact with Justin.

He released her hand, took a glass of champagne from a passing tray and handed it to her. "Thank you for coming. Enjoy the party," he said. He then excused himself and turned to resume his conversation with some of the other guests. Sylvia started to walk away, when she felt a hand touch her arm.

"I see you changed your mind." Sylvia turned and looked squarely into the face of Paul Wright.

"Not completely," she said a little sheepishly. "I did attend the concert." Her face burned with embarrassment as she realized Paul was aware of her inability to keep her eyes from straying to the extremely handsome Justin Udall. He searched her face and slowly his lips pulled into a knowing smile. Taking her by the hand, he walked over to the group where the young artist was monopolizing a conversation. She was pleased with his action, for it gave her the opportunity to better scrutinize Justin's good looks. His six-foot six-inch lean frame and dark brown complexion seemed expressly made for the formal evening attire he wore.

"You haven't thanked me yet for sending Sylvia to your studio today," Paul said, interrupting the conversation.

Justin smiled and turned to look at them as Sylvia's eyes quickly swept over him, noting classic features, even white teeth, dark expressive eyes, slightly long, curly hair that caressed the collar of his ruffled shirt and a hypnotic smile.

"Thank you, Paul, for sending such a lovely young lady into my life." Justin's expression was unreadable, but for a moment Sylvia wondered if she had detected a note of sarcasm in his deep voice. "Please excuse me," he said again, and walked away to join an elderly couple seated on a sofa. As he sat down beside them, Sylvia noticed the shoes he wore were not the traditional slippers worn with evening attire, but instead were a pair of black rattlesnake cowboy boots.

"He's a little eccentric," Paul commented, when he saw her eyes fasten on Justin's boots.

"It appears that way," she responded.

The evening waned, as Sylvia mingled with different guests at the party. Several times during the evening she noticed Polly staring at her. Shortly after midnight, Paul gave Sylvia a ride to her hotel.

Chapter Two

As Sylvia drove down Richmond Road to work, her thoughts centered on Justin Udall. Never before had she met anyone who had made such a profound impression on her in so short a period of time. Her mind went blank, as she attempted to recall what they had talked about at the party. What had he said? As far as that mattered, what had she said? She thought hard for several minutes before answering her question. Nothing. Well, almost nothing. The little bit he had said to her had been perfunctory and almost rude. He certainly hadn't seemed overjoyed that she had bought thirteen of his works earlier that day. She wondered if he was superstitious like his friend, and then dismissed the idea. He just didn't seem the type.

She made a left turn onto South Post Oak Road, drove a block before making a right turn onto Alabama Street, and parked her car in the lot on the corner. *Perhaps*, she said to herself, still trying to answer the question burning inside her, *I can't get Justin out of my mind because his work is so fantastic*. However, as she got out of the car and walked toward Emary Oaks, the image of Justin in his formal attire lingered in her thoughts. Just maybe she couldn't dismiss Justin from her mind because she had been so very attracted to his incredible good looks. She chuckled to herself as she entered the store and made her way to the escalators. *How silly,* she thought. *Surely, I'm thinking of Justin only because I know his work will bring new excitement to the shop.* At the third floor, she got off the escalator and walked through a set of white double doors.

"Good morning," Sylvia spoke to her boss, Henrika Hagen, as she entered their small, cluttered office. "I have terrific news."

"Great," Henrika answered, not looking up from her desk. "I can always use good news on a Monday morning." Her blond head rose slowly from her work and with sparkling green eyes she peered expectantly at Sylvia.

"I've found an extremely talented artist in Dallas whose work is simply fantastic," Sylvia announced. "I bought twelve of his canvases. They should arrive in a couple of days."

"Oh, Sylvia," Henrika moaned in dismay, "that wasn't a very wise thing to do." Rising from her chair, she walked to the window and looked out at the giant oak trees standing sentry at the entrance to Emary Oaks. "Why so many?"

"I told you, Henrika, his work is extraordinary."

"He's an unknown."

"Yes, but not for long," Sylvia said matter-of-factly. "Don't worry. We'll sell all of the canvases by Christmas."

"I hope so," Henrika said. "Paintings, especially by an unknown, are a very tricky commodity to sell. Who is he?" She turned to look directly at Sylvia.

"Justin Udall. He's a native Texan and I bought seven of his pen and ink drawings, three water colors and two oil paintings."

"Oil paintings and water colors! Were they expensive?"

"Very," Sylvia answered, laughing at the exasperated expression that had crept onto Henrika's face. "But I'm taking them on consignment."

"That's a relief," Henrika sighed. "If I thought for a moment I could get along without you, Sylvia," she teased, "I'd throw you out of here on your ear for giving me such a scare."

"Let's face it, Henrika," Sylvia countered with the same tone in her voice, "if you weren't married to the owner of Emary Oaks, we both would've been thrown out a long time ago for taking outrageous risks." They laughed conspiratorially as they settled down to their work.

"The funny thing is," Henrika said, turning once more to look at Sylvia, "those outrageous chances have always turned into outrageous profits."

"I know," Sylvia replied, "and the Justin Udall works are such an outrageous risk that I'm sure they'll put Emary Oaks on the map." Again a mass of giggles erupted from their throats and filled the small office. The two women worked well together, and though Henrika was ten years older than Sylvia, over the years they had grown to be very good friends.

Sylvia spent the day working in the office. Advertising copy needed her approval for the Sunday papers. New items had arrived that needed pricing for resale. She had a short staff meeting with the two saleswomen in her department to introduce the new stock. Several invoices needed her authorization for payment, and some damaged merchandise had to be returned to the manufacturers.

At the end of the day, she called her best friend, Bluma Hume, and invited her to her condominium for dinner.

"How was Dallas?" Bluma asked, helping Sylvia clear away the dishes.

"Very interesting," Sylvia replied. "I found some good buys for the shop, had lunch with Paul, attended a concert and," unconsciously she drew in a deep breath and expelled it dreamily, "I met Justin Udall."

Bluma folded the dish towel neatly and hung it on a rack to dry. "Sounds like Paul has finally introduced you to Mr. Right."

"Don't be silly, girl," Sylvia said, surprised at her friend's statement. "How can you conclude such a thing when I only said I *met* Justin Udall." She led the way into the living room carrying a couple of glasses of minted iced tea. "Anyway, he was not one of Paul's fix-ups, though he and Paul are very good friends," she explained. "Justin Udall is this exceptionally-talented artist who has a studio in Dallas. I bought twelve of his canvases for the shop and one for myself. My only interest in the man is his work." She handed a glass to her friend, feeling quite satisfied with the explanation she had offered.

But Sylvia could not deny to herself that thoughts of Justin had roamed around in her head all morning. Each time she felt she had successfully pushed him out of one corner of her mind, he had reemerged in another. It had been a constant battle. Nevertheless, she certainly had not, at any time, considered him to be Mr. Right in any form or fashion, she told herself. She only felt he was a very talented, attractive man. Her finger carefully traced the rim of her glass. What had Bluma thought she detected in her voice or saw in her face that had caused her to make such a statement? Quickly, she stole a look at her friend. Bluma had neither seen nor heard anything, she decided. She was just guessing.

"Um hmm," Bluma said thoughtfully. She sat on the bright red sofa and tucked her slim, shapely legs underneath her. For a moment, a frown creased her pretty, chocolate-colored face. "What's he like?" she asked, playing with a lock of her short, curly hair.

Sylvia sipped slowly from her glass of iced tea. "He's thirty-five years old, extremely handsome and taller than me." To her embarrassment, she realized the information she had so eagerly supplied clearly conveyed that she had given considerable thought to Justin's physical and personal attributes. "He's physically attractive as well as a tremendous talent," she added quickly. "Facts are facts."

"Of course." They eyed each other for a few seconds before Bluma spoke again. "Well, I'm sorry if I upset you by suggesting you're interested in this man for reasons other than his art," she said smiling. "I guess I just *imagined* I saw a certain light in your eyes when you mentioned his name."

Sylvia blushed. "You-are-wrong!" she emphasized.

"Hmph." Bluma cleared her throat as she looked at Sylvia disbelievingly. She set her glass aside and stretched her legs out in front of her. "How is Armand?" she asked.

"He's fine," Sylvia said of her fiance. "As a matter of

fact, I'm supposed to have dinner with him tomorrow."

Bluma looked at her friend knowingly. "Have you set your wedding date yet?"

Her questions made Sylvia uneasy, for they broached a subject she didn't want to discuss. Besides, why had she mentioned Armand when they were discussing Justin and his work? What was her point?

"No," Sylvia answered, taking their glasses to the kitchen. She rinsed them out and set them on the drain. "I can't seem to make up my mind whether I want to get married in the winter or the spring." She walked back into the living room and plopped into a chair.

"Maybe this fantastic artist guy will help you make a decision."

Sylvia laughed lightheartedly. "Will you stop! He can't help me do anything but make money for the Nook of International Treasures with his art."

"I doubt it." She picked up her things to leave. "I can see you're very much attracted to the man."

"I just met him."

Bluma walked to the door and paused to look at her friend. "That's all it takes in some cases, and" she said pointing her finger teasingly, "that's how it's happened for you with Mr. Fantastic Artist."

"Good-bye, Bluma," Sylvia said, ignoring her friend's remark.

"We'll see. I'll call you for lunch next week," Bluma said as she walked out the door.

Sylvia closed the door and sank onto the sofa. Bluma had always been able to read her emotions, even when she was unable or unwilling to decipher them herself. However, in this case, she was sure her dear friend was wrong about her feelings for Justin Udall. She hardly knew the man. She found him attractive and extremely talented, but that was all.

Later that night as Sylvia prepared her bath, she chided herself for allowing Bluma's observations to cause her to doubt her own mind. She liked Armand a great deal and probably would marry him. But—she didn't like admitting it—she *was* having difficulty setting a date for their marriage. She realized that she would have to tell Bluma and Paul in no uncertain terms that Armand was the right man for her and that she *would* set their wedding date soon. Paul and Bluma would have to accept the fact that she was capable of making her own decisions.

She lathered herself swiftly and slowly rinsed the soap from her body. Her mind rambled to Armand Blandon, whom she had known most of her life. They had grown up together in Houston, and both had chosen to attend college in New York City. During that time they saw each other often, but their relationship never developed beyond that of a close friendship. It was not until four months ago that Armand had professed his love and asked her to be his wife. Sylvia had been surprised by his confession, but promised to give him her answer in a few days. The days had stretched into weeks and then into months. Armand had received his doctorate degree in chemistry in June and had landed an excellent job with one of the large oil companies in the city. Now he was anxious to get married. Since she had not rejected his proposal, he had assumed her answer was 'yes' and had begun pressing her to set a date for their wedding.

Paul had begun his campaign for finding a suitable mate for her *after* she had told him Armand had asked her to be his wife, she remembered as she stepped out of her bath and dried herself briskly with a large bath towel. He had met Armand on several occasions and had later told Sylvia he felt she would be making a grave mistake if she married him.

Sylvia slipped a short cotton nightie over her head, set her alarm clock and crawled into bed. For most of the night, she slept peacefully. Toward morning, however, she drifted into a disturbing dream where she was being chased by Armand with a diamond engagement ring the size of an egg. She was running away from him along a winding path with all the speed she could muster, with Bluma on the sideline cheering her on. She could hear her friend yelling, "You can do it, Sylvia, you can do it!" As she rounded a curve in the path, she ran into a tall, dark figure who caught her in his arms and said to her, "You can stop running now, you're safe." She looked up into the figure's face and recognized Justin Udall's hypnotic smile. The alarm clock sounded, causing Sylvia to bolt upright in bed. Groggily, she roused herself and dressed for work.

Although her day was pleasant and full of duties she enjoyed, Sylvia had difficulty keeping thoughts of her early morning dream from plaguing her. She sat at her desk wondering if her subconscious mind was trying to reveal some truth to her that she was afraid to face. If so, what? Why was she running away from Armand, and why was he chasing her with such a huge ring? Had Justin Udall been in the dream? Had he held her in his arms and told her she was safe? Safe from what? Surely not Armand. Dear, sweet Armand would never hurt anyone, she thought.

She got to her feet and walked over to the window. The dream just didn't make sense, especially the chasing part. She wanted to marry Armand and would set their wedding date soon. As she watched customers enter and leave the store, a smile pulled at her lips. One part of the dream had made sense. Bluma had been in character. She *would* cheer if Sylvia ran away from Armand. She had always been against their marriage.

Sylvia pulled herself from the window and forced her thoughts back to the work on her desk. She managed to get through the day with minimal problems. In the late evening, she left Emary Oaks for home.

. After a quick bath, Sylvia slipped into a white crepe de chine dress with tiny shoulder straps, a fitted bodice and a full mid-calf length skirt. She applied makeup lightly over her face, pulled her hair into a tight chignon, and stepped into a pair of satin, high-heeled champagne-colored sandals. The door bell chimed just as she hung a small, white beaded bag over her shoulder. Sylvia dabbed perfume on her skin and opened the door for Armand.

"Baby, you look beautiful, as usual," Armand said, stepping inside and stretching up to peck her on the cheek. She bent slightly forward to accommodate him.

"Thank you," Sylvia replied, smiling at him affectionately as they walked out the door. "Where will we have dinner?" she asked, as he guided her out to his blue Volvo and helped her into the car.

"I've found a nice little restaurant out Richmond Road that I think you'll like. The food is very good. I hope you're hungry."

"I am," she assured him.

When they arrived at the restaurant, they were taken to their table without delay. The room was small and cozy and dimly lit. A violinist wandered among the tables, playing familiar romantic songs. Sylvia liked the place, and immediately her spirits lifted in anticipation of having an enjoyable evening.

After Armand had ordered them a meal of fish chowder, veal scallops with mushrooms, romaine with watercress dressing, rolls, a dry white wine, fresh peach cake and coffee, they settled back and began catching up on the events that had occurred in each other's lives since they had last seen each other.

"I'm glad to hear your trip to Dallas was so successful," Armand said, when she had finished telling him about all the wonderful items she had found for the shop. "Both of our professional lives are going so well, don't you think it's about time we started talking about our personal lives? When can we start making plans for our wedding?"

Sylvia's heart jumped as, for some strange reason, thoughts of her dream flashed through her head. "I don't think we should rush into anything, Armand," she answered uneasily, attempting to avoid the subject. She smiled across the table at him. He was not the man she had dreamed of marrying when she was a little girl. But what little girl ever grew up and married her dream man? She knew that Armand was the right man for her. He was gentle and kind, and gave her enough room to be herself. She liked him a lot, and always felt safe with him. She enjoyed their times together. Furthermore, her family, particularly her Aunt Bea, was fond of

Armand and looked forward to their wedding day.

A confused expression crossed Armand's thin brown face. "I don't understand," he said disconcertedly.

Sylvia nervously stirred her soup, which the waiter had just served. How could she explain to him something she didn't understand herself? She had convinced herself that marrying Armand was the best thing for her, so why was she reluctant to discuss wedding plans? "There's no need to rush and make plans," she finally said, choosing her words carefully. "I think I'd like to be a spring bride. We have all winter to make arrangements."

Armand's expression changed to one of relief and happiness. "Well, I can understand your wanting to get married in the spring, honey, but you know how much I love you and I'm not sure I want to wait that long to make you my wife."

Sylvia blushed and smiled warmly at him. Armand was so very trusting and understanding. "I would wait for *you*," she responded coyly.

When Armand reached over and took her hands in his and kissed them gently, Sylvia knew that, for the present time, they would let the subject drop. As she watched him from under her lashes, she thought of how lucky she was to be marrying a man with such fine qualities.

The waiter brought the main course and they chatted congenially as they completed their meal. Since they both had heavy work schedules the following day, they agreed to end the evening early.

* * *

On Wednesday morning, the shipment came in from the Udall studio. Sylvia unpacked the paintings and began pricing them for resale. After sticking the prices to the back of the canvases, she placed them around the small office. She was trying to decide how she would arrange them in the shop, when Henrika entered the room.

"They're here," Sylvia announced, when she saw her.

Henrika walked to each canvas and examined it carefully. It was the first time she seemed so taken by items that had been bought for the Nook of International Treasures. After a few minutes, she picked up the two oil paintings and took them to her desk.

"I'm buying these for myself," she said casually. "Sylvia," she added, turning to the young woman who was looking at her with an `I told you so' expression, "you were right as usual. He *is* fantastic."

"I know," Sylvia said gathering up the remaining canvases. "I think I'll get these on the floor before there are none left for the customers."

"You'd better hurry," Henrika told her, "because I have my eye on that water color in your hand."

Sylvia laughed and took the canvases out to display them. The Nook of International Treasures was the size of a small room, and was situated in the middle of the third floor of the store. Elegant and interesting art items were placed strategically within the area, giving it the air of a splendid, multicultured wonderland. Sylvia arranged the canvases carefully, and for a couple of hours she worked with Mary, one of the saleswomen, selling in the shop. The Udall works generated a great deal of interest. Sylvia talked with customers at length about the artist and his work. At two o'clock, when she decided to take her lunch break, four of the canvases had been sold. By the end of the day, only three were left.

On Thursday morning, Paul called to give Sylvia more leads for finding additional native Texas arts and crafts. She took the information down and made a tentative buying schedule for the following two weeks, realizing that she would have to travel throughout the state to find the items she needed for her special holiday project.

"What's the possibility of getting more Udall canvases?" Henrika asked, coming into the office. "I've just sold the last one."

"I'm not sure," Sylvia answered, "but I can call his studio and find out."

"Please try," Henrika sighed. "Two little ladies left here angry because they couldn't at least view the works of the artist they'd heard so much about."

"How could they have heard so much about Justin Udall's works?" Sylvia asked. "We've only had them since yesterday."

"I know," Henrika said, stepping out of her shoes and wiggling her toes. "It seems he was discussed thoroughly at some grand dinner party last night." She stepped back into her shoes. "And that means it's just a matter of time before others come in asking for his canvases. I'd like to have something here for them to see."

"I told you he would put Emary Oaks on the map," Sylvia laughed good-naturedly.

"You were right as always," Henrika said, joining Sylvia in laughter. "And since you seem to have the Midas touch, I'd like you to go to his studio and choose the canvases for us. His works have brought a lot of excitement to the shop and that's very good for business."

Sylvia called Athena DeForest late Thursday and told her how successfully the works had sold. She informed Athena that she would like to return to the studio on Friday morning to look at more canvases for the Nook of International Treasures. Athena was very excited about the success of her brother's work and asked Sylvia to come to the studio before one o'clock because she and Justin had planned to have lunch together at that time. She invited Sylvia to join them.

Chapter Three

Dressed in a beige classic silk suit with a complimentary white silk shirt and taupe high-heeled leather sandals, Sylvia left her hotel for the Udall studio. Her fingers toyed nervously with a string of opera-length cultured pearls, which perfectly matched the stud earrings she wore, as the taxi made its way through the busy Dallas avenues. She no longer tried to deny that she was eagerly looking forward to seeing Justin Udall again. She told herself, however, that her excitement stemmed from the realization that their business association would, no doubt, generate huge profits for both of them. Surely it could be nothing more. She held fast to her conviction that Bluma had been wrong in her observations.

Absently, she gazed out of the window and found herself mentally comparing Justin Udall and Armand Blandon. How silly, she gently reprimanded herself, you don't know enough about Justin Udall to compare him with anyone. Why then, had Armand not measured up to him? She laughed to herself as the cab pulled in front of the studio. You must get things into perspective, Sylvia, she told herself. This is to be a business lunch, not some rendezvous with a new love. She paid the driver and entered the studio.

"It's so good to see you again, Sylvia," Athena said, embracing her. "Did you have a good flight?"

"I had a very pleasant flight," Sylvia replied, returning Athena's warm greeting. "And it's wonderful to be back under such exciting circumstances."

"I couldn't believe it when you called yesterday to say all of Justin's canvases had been sold. It was like a dream come true."

"I can imagine," Sylvia agreed, "and I'm hoping you'll consider the Nook of International Treasures as your Houston outlet for Justin's work in your plans for the future."

"Oh, I'm sure that can be arranged," Athena said, obviously pleased.

A soft, feminine cough brought the conversation to an abrupt pause. Athena's face flushed. "Oh, I'm sorry," she said, turning to look at Polly who had come over to join them from another part of the studio. "I became so excited over the success of Justin's work that I've neglected you, Polly." She turned back to Sylvia. "You met Polly Vance at my dinner party," she said. "She's joining us for lunch."

"How nice," Sylvia replied, fighting a wave of disappointment. Sylvia and Polly eyed each other coolly.

"Justin won't be able to join us," Athena announced. "He's working in his studio out at the ranch and decided not to drive into the city today. He sends his apologies."

Acute disappointment gripped Sylvia, but she managed to smile and find her voice. "Maybe next time," she said smoothly.

Athena looked at her curiously before picking up her

handbag and walking to the door. "I've made reserva-
tions for us at the little French restaurant around the
corner. Shall we go?"

The small, elegant restaurant was attractively decorated with potted plants, heavy drapes and mirrors. It
was quite crowded, Sylvia noticed as they were led to a
table. Athena suggested they order quiche and soup,
and the two women agreed.

"I haven't told Justin about the success of his work at
Emary Oaks yet," Athena began. "I had planned to let
you tell him today, Sylvia."

"I would have loved that. If Justin comes into Dallas
one day this weekend, maybe I can talk to him then."
Sylvia smiled and brightened at the possibility of seeing
him before going back to Houston.

"Justin intends to work at the ranch all weekend,"
Polly interjected, looking at Sylvia with daggers in her
eyes.

For a moment Sylvia was stunned by the bitterness in
Polly's voice. Why was she so protective of Justin?
Was she his agent? His fiancee? Suppose she was. Why
would she want to protect him from her? After all, she
was interested in buying and promoting his work.
Nothing more. But Polly had acted the same way when
she had first met her at Athena's party. She had sensed
the instant animosity. Why? Certainly she hadn't
thought Sylvia was interested in Justin and not his art.
That was absurd. The night of the party was the first
time she had met the man. I won't allow Polly to
interfere with my buying Justin's work, she thought. If
she's his agent, let her speak up and give me the terms
under which she'll sell to Emary Oaks, otherwise I'll
just ignore her little nasty comments. She turned her

attention back to Athena. "Does he work there often?" she asked, speaking directly to Athena.

Athena opened her mouth to answer, but Polly, determined not to be squeezed out of the conversation, spoke first. "Yes," she said quickly, "he does most of his work at the ranch these days."

"He seems to draw inspiration from the country," Athena added, her eyes full of compassion for Polly. "He has done some exciting canvases since he's been working there."

"I'd like to see them," Sylvia said.

For a moment Athena was reflective. "I'm leaving this evening to spend the weekend at the ranch, Sylvia," she told her. "Why don't you come with me? Then you'll have the perfect opportunity to talk with Justin at length about his work."

"That sounds wonderful. "I would love it," Sylvia was elated.

"But Athena ..." Polly began.

"I would invite you also, Polly," she added, "but I know you're leaving for Washington, D.C. tonight to visit your parents."

Sylvia was very pleased with the way events were developing. The invitation to the ranch and the news of Polly leaving the city caused her spirits to lift. She realized, too, that her reasons for not wanting Polly around for the weekend had nothing whatsoever to do with buying Justin's work for the Nook of International Treasures. Polly had forced her to be true to herself. She was interested in Justin Udall for more reasons than his art. Bluma had been right all along.

"You're visiting your parents this weekend," Sylvia said, smiling coolly. "How nice." She turned to look at a pouting Polly. "Do have a safe trip," she offered triumphantly.

Polly's face was flushed with anger. "I don't think you should allow Sylvia to disturb Justin's work," she argued. "I'm sure he's at the ranch this weekend because he wants solitude." The women had completed their lunch and were waiting for the check.

"If Justin doesn't want to talk with Sylvia about his work or show her his canvases, Polly," Athena said firmly, "I'm sure he won't hesitate to say so. Enjoy your vacation and don't fret about Justin. He can take care of himself."

"You're right, Athena," Polly said sweetly, regaining her composure. "Forgive me for doubting your judgment."

"All is forgiven," Athena said with a smile.

After leaving the restaurant, they walked leisurely back to the studio. "You know, Sylvia," Polly spoke in the same sugar-coated voice she had used earlier, "you remind me of a giant that I once read about in a fairy tale when I was a little girl. He was terribly frightening to little old ladies and small children. They would run from him. Even their little pet kittens and rabbits would scuttle for safety when they saw him coming. I'll bet—because of your height, of course—you frighten little old ladies and small children, too." She sighed sympathetically. "I must admit that I'm comfortable with you now only because Athena is here with us. Otherwise, I'm afraid I would find you most frightening."

"Polly!" Athena gasped in disbelief. "How awful!"

Sylvia began to laugh, and laughed so hard and long, tears rolled down her cheeks and she held her sides. Polly and Athena watched her nervously. "Don't look so worried, Polly," she finally said when she was able to get her breath. "I don't find your observations offensive at all. But," she added, wiping tears from her face, "I would imagine that you also find Justin `most frightening'." She waited for Polly to reply.

"Of course I'm not afraid of Justin," she snapped and resumed her walking.

"He's pretty tall," Sylvia reminded her.

"Tall men aren't as frightening as tall women," Polly informed the beautiful young woman, as they followed Athena into the studio.

"I see," Sylvia laughed. "But wasn't the giant a man?"

Polly glared at her as she headed for the restroom to freshen up. After choosing several canvases to be sold at the Nook of International Treasures, Sylvia left Athena and Polly at the studio with the understanding that Athena would pick her up in the late afternoon at her hotel. She then went shopping to buy items she felt she would need for a weekend at the ranch. After making her purchases, she went back to the hotel and packed.

Late afternoon, Athena picked Sylvia up at her hotel, and they set out for the ranch. As they drove, Sylvia was tempted several times to ask Athena about Polly's relationship to Justin. However, she suppressed her curiosity and confined her conversation to chatting about Emary Oaks.

They reached the ranch after driving an hour and a half through gently rolling, semi-wooded farmland,

and past several cattle ranches strung along the high-way.

"Is this all yours?" Sylvia asked with awe, as Athena pulled the steel-gray Mercedes into the driveway.

Athena glanced at her, her eyes filled with pride. "Yes," she answered softly. "It was left to Justin and me by our grandfather several years ago. Come," she said getting out of the car, "let's go inside. You've had a tiring day."

Sylvia followed Athena into the house where Copland, Athena's husband, was waiting for them. "You ladies got here just in time," his robust voice filled the room. "I was just preparing one of my favorite menus. I hope you're hungry."

"That was sweet of you," Athena said, kissing him lightly on the cheek. "You do remember Sylvia, don't you?" she asked.

"Of course, I do. Welcome to the ranch, Sylvia," Copland grinned as he reached for her bags. "I'll take these to your room, and Athena can get you settled in while I finish with dinner. It should be ready in about half an hour."

Sylvia followed them to a room at the end of a hallway. After they had left, she unpacked, changed for dinner and, following directions Athena had given her, made her way back to the dining room.

"Everything looks scrumptious, like a page out of a magazine," Sylvia remarked, when she saw the meal Copland had prepared for them.

"Thank you," Copland beamed as he took a low bow. "Now, dig right in. I hope you don't mind our informal-ity."

"Here at the ranch, we're quite informal," Athena

chimed in.

They were serving themselves when Justin, clad in snug jeans, a fine white cotton cowboy shirt with multicolored hand embroidery, and a pair of well-worn brown cowboy boots, joined them. "Sorry, I'm late," he said, entering the room with easy, cat-like strides. He sat in the chair across from Sylvia. "It's good to see you again, Lovely Lady," he greeted her.

"Thank you." Sylvia tried to hide a blush. "It was generous of Athena to invite me here for the weekend." Under Justin's steady gaze, she felt nervous and self-conscious.

"It was kind of you to agree to spend the weekend with us at the last minute," Athena said. "Sylvia had planned to spend her time in Dallas," Athena informed her brother.

Justin, allowing his dark, expressive eyes to gently caress Sylvia's face, spoke in a serious tone. "She looks too much like a city mouse to enjoy a weekend in the country," he said, winking at Athena.

"Oh, I love the country," Sylvia heard herself say much too defensively. Embarrassed, she dropped her eyes to her plate and tried to ignore Justin's gaze boring into her flesh.

"In that case," he said, a smile pulling at the corner of his mouth, "we should all have a lovely weekend."

Sylvia concentrated on her dinner, feeling she had conveyed too much interest in the man and not his art. She silently reminded herself of her primary reason for coming to Dallas in the first place. Dinner progressed and she found herself enjoying both the meal and her companions.

"Sylvia came to town for a very special reason,"

Athena announced proudly as they conversed.

"And what reason is that?" Copland asked. He turned large brown eyes set in a pleasant olive-brown face to Sylvia.

"Your canvases have caused quite a stir in Houston," Sylvia said to Justin. "I came back this weekend to purchase more of your work."

"She chose twenty wonderful canvases today," Athena added. "I'll send them to the store on Monday."

"You two have been very busy," Justin said drily. He swallowed the last of his wine and turned to his brother-in-law. "Thanks for dinner," he said, getting up from his chair.

Athena was perplexed by Justin's behavior. "The news doesn't please you?" she asked.

"Not particularly," he said acrimoniously. "Please excuse me." He walked to the door and Sylvia's eyes followed him.

"I'm sorry if I've insulted you by selling your work," she said. Her annoyance was apparent in her voice. "I apologize."

"Apology accepted, Lovely Lady," he replied, and left the room.

Angry and confused, Sylvia turned to Athena and Copland for an answer. The expressions on their faces showed they were just as bewildered as she was by Justin's behavior.

"I ...I'm sorry," Athena stammered. "I don't understand why he's acting this way." She turned to her husband.

"Neither do I," he said, shrugging his shoulders. "It sounded like great news to me."

Athena rose from her chair and began clearing the

table. "Justin is simply impossible sometimes," she said angrily. She picked up dishes of food and started for the kitchen. Sylvia followed her with a stack of plates and some silverware.

"Perhaps I shouldn't have come," she said. "But I thought giving him the news about his work would please him."

"One would think so," Athena replied. "And why should your coming here to tell him that his work has been well received in Houston cause him to act as if he has never been introduced to common courtesy and good sense? He's impossible," she mumbled to herself.

They finished cleaning the kitchen and went to the living room where they found Justin and Copland engaged in conversation. Sylvia hesitated for a moment when she saw Justin turn and give her a thorough onceover and then abruptly turn away.

"I promised Sylvia she would have an opportunity to talk with you about your work this weekend, Justin," Athena said, interrupting them. "Will that be possible?" she added with sarcasm. Sylvia grew more uncomfortable. But, under the circumstances, she was relieved to get the proposal out in the open.

"I'd be delighted to discuss my work with the Lovely Lady," Justin said, getting up from the sofa and walking over to Sylvia. "Why don't we go out to my studio now?" A broad smile crossed his face as he offered her his arm. Taking it, Sylvia could feel her anger subside, and again she grew optimistic about the weekend.

"You're certainly full of surprises today, Justin," Athena said, shaking her head.

"You are too, sister dear," he replied, "and this is one suprise that I truly appreciate." He unlocked his arm from Sylvia's and slid it casually around her slender waist. As he guided her out of the house and down the short tree-lined path to his studio, Sylvia felt his grip tighten. Involuntarily, a shudder shot down her spine.

Once inside the studio, she was surprised to see that Justin was now working in only one medium—water colors. The canvases were just as exciting as ever. "I simply love your work," she said, walking from one canvas to another.

"Thank you."

"Why are you working only in water colors now?"

"It suits me."

"I see." She walked to a stool and sat down. "Some of my customers have wanted to know more about you than is written in your brochures."

"Your customers?"

"Yes." Sylvia was angered by his insinuation, but she didn't want to flare up again. She began admiring a canvas of gnarled trees.

Justin deliberately walked between the painting that she was admiring and her line of vision and sprawled on a small bench against a wall. "I've studied in Italy and Mexico, as well as here in Texas." He spoke matter-of-factly. "I earned a Ph.D. in Art at the University of Texas, and I've taught art here at the university in Dallas for the past five years. I've painted seriously," he continued, "since the age of fifteen. And now, after twenty years of study and work, I'm painting full time and enjoying it very much." Abruptly he got up, walked to the door and waited for her to join him. "End of interview, Lovely Lady," he said. He escorted her out of the studio and locked the door behind them. She had learned exactly nothing new. Well, at least she had seen his new work.

A warm breeze stirred as they stood on the path between the studio and the rambling ranch house. The grassland that stretched before them seemed to go on endlessly, reaching out to a slowly setting sun. Justin took Sylvia's hand in his and began walking toward the horizon. "So you like the country," he said, after they had walked for a while. He released her hand and stuffed both of his in his back jean pockets.

Sylvia could feel her blood pressure return to normal. "I love the country," she replied, pulling a stalk of grass from the ground and sticking it between her teeth.

"You've been watching too much T.V.," Justin said, eyeing her.

"I know," she laughed after realizing what she had done. "I watch a lot of old westerns."

"Me too," he confessed.

When they had walked about half a mile from the back of the house, they came to a fence that bordered the limitless fields. Sylvia quickly climbed it and perched on its top. "I love sunsets too," she said, looking into the distance.

"Is that a fact?" Justin climbed the fence and sat next to her.

"That's a fact." She turned and smiled at him, and became too aware of his overwhelming magnetism. She felt herself unwillingly drawn to him. "Do you know what's needed to complete this scene?" she asked.

"A horse?"

"No. Music." She began singing a country and western song and making elaborate gestures. Justin joined in, trying to harmonize with her, and they both began to laugh. They laughed so hard, Sylvia lost her balance. Justin tried to catch her as she slipped, and they both fell to the ground. They lay on their backs in the dewy grass, laughing hysterically.

"Know what?" Sylvia asked, still laughing hard.

"What?"

"You can't sing," she informed him.

"I know," he said. Justin suddenly stopped laughing and a serious expression crossed his face. He rolled over and propped his head up with one hand, as he reached over and cupped Sylvia's chin in the other. "I know something else," he said hoarsely, looking deeply into her eyes. "You're a lovely, lovely lady." He slowly moved his face toward hers. Sylvia lay motionless as he began dotting her forehead, eyelids, nose, cheeks, ears and neck with light kisses. He moved over her, his large masterful hands slowly caressing her face and shoulders as his warm mouth found hers and deeply probed her parted lips. Inflamed, Sylvia pushed him away. Slowly, Justin got to his feet and reached out a hand to help her get up. "Problem?" he asked, flashing his hypnotic smile.

"No, no problem," she lied, visibly shaken by her body's involuntary response to his kisses. Silently they walked back to the house and joined Athena and Copland in the living room.

The next morning, Athena took Sylvia on a guided tour of the ranch by horseback. She pointed out places where she and Justin had played as children. Sylvia fell in love with one particular area that was peppered with a variety of oak and pine trees, surrounding a very inviting creek which Athena assured her was the best place around for swimming. Athena proudly talked about Grandpa Udall, from whom they had inherited the ranch. "As a young man," she said solemnly, "he bought several hundred acres of land scattered around the Houston/Dallas areas. But ten years ago, he was forced to sell to land developers. Soon after that he died. I'll always believe that the loss of his land killed him."

"I'm sorry," Sylvia said awkwardly.

"Oh, I guess it couldn't be helped," Athena continued. "The cities had begun to spread out and one old man couldn't stand in the path of progress. Anyway, Justin and I were able to make some lucrative investments with the proceeds from the sales. I think Grandpa would've been proud. Our grandparents spent all of their married life here on this 500 acre track of land," she said, "and I'm glad Justin and I have agreed that it will never be sold."

Shortly before noon, they turned their horses and headed back to the house. After a brief swim in the pool, Athena and Sylvia prepared lunch and ate by the pool side. They were lolling contentedly, when Copland joined them.

"Did you tell Sylvia about the party this evening, hon? You know Mike and Sandy will be disappointed if we don't show," he said to Athena, as he settled into a lounge chair.

"Oh Cop, you know I completely forgot about it. Are you interested in attending a barbeque and pool party our neighbors are having this evening?" Athena asked, addressing Sylvia. "We accepted the invitation weeks ago and I'm afraid there's no way we can get out of it.

I'm sorry I didn't mention it earlier. I'm sure you'll like Mike and Sandy. They're a lot of fun."

"I'd love to," Sylvia accepted.

Shortly after two o'clock, Sylvia went to her room to rest before going to the party. She lay in bed thinking about Justin and remembering his tender kisses of the previous day. Recalling the intense, tingling sensations she had experienced when he had caressed her and his sensuous lips had met hers, she wondered where he was and why she hadn't seen him all day. The only thing she really knew about Justin was what she knew of his work. Was he involved with a woman? What about Polly? At least now she was fairly certain Polly was not his agent. But what was her relationship with him? She had to find out.

She closed her eyes and a warm sensation flowed through her body as she clung to the memory of his deep, probing kisses. His work was probably his first love, she thought. But what, or who, was his second love? Polly? She fluffed her pillow vigorously and settled on her side. What do you care, Sylvia, she scolded herself. You're going to marry Armand Blandon next spring. What Justin does with his personal life is his affair. But, she thought, she would never allow him to kiss or hold her in his arms again. Justin was no doubt used to having any woman he desired, but she would not be his plaything. If Polly was involved with Justin, she could relax. All she wanted from him was his art to sell at Emary Oaks. Before long, she rolled back onto her stomach and drifted off to sleep.

When she woke up a couple of hours later, Sylvia felt refreshed and ready for the party. She showered, pulled her hair back into a tight knot and slipped into a pair of short khaki shorts and a white tank top. She packed her swim suit, a towel, and other necessities in a tote bag, stepped into a pair of brown canvas sandals, and went to the living room.

"Oh, there you are," Athena said, putting aside the magazine she was reading. "Did you rest well?"

"Yes, thank you," Sylvia replied, looking about for Justin. There was no trace of him. "Where's Copland?" she asked.

"Out front waiting for us."

"I hope I'm not late," Sylvia said, following Athena out of the house.

"You're right on time," Athena reassured her. They walked to the car and Sylvia's heart began to throb when she saw Justin sitting in the driver's seat. Copland, who was sitting in the passenger seat, got out and helped them into the back seat of the car.

"So, how are you enjoying your weekend?" Justin asked, waiting for them to settle themselves.

"I'm enjoying it very much," Sylvia answered, as Justin started the car, drove down the long driveway and pulled onto the road. "Athena gave me a tour of the ranch this morning and I'm afraid I've fallen in love with it. Especially the creek."

"Oh yes, the creek," Justin said. "Great place for skinny-dipping."

"Justin!" Athena's tone cautioned him.

Copland laughed softly. "Don't embarrass your sister, Justin," he said.

"I'm only stating the truth," Justin insisted. "Creeks are made for swimming—but only if you're nude. It's good therapy for your mental health. Ask any doctor," he eyed Athena, "or retired nurse."

Athena's lips pulled into a smile in spite of herself. "I think you should have started your weekend with a ten minute swim there," she informed him.

They were all laughing when Justin pulled into the driveway of the neighboring ranch. They got out of the car and followed the pungent, smoky odor of grilled beef around the side of the house to the pool, where they found their hosts, Mike and Sandy, lolling with a small group of people.

"Hi there," Mike said, getting up to greet them. "We thought you had changed your minds and decided not to come."

"We wouldn't do that," Copland said, shaking his friend's hand. "This is Sylvia Random, our guest for the weekend. We knew you wouldn't mind if we brought her along."

"It's good to meet you, Sylvia," Mike said. "A beautiful young lady is always a welcome guest in our home." He introduced everyone.

"Let me show you where to change," Sandy said, leading the way to the bathhouse. She was a short, chubby woman with red hair, blue eyes and a friendly smile. "I'm so glad you came," she added, turning to Athena. "Now the evening will be perfect."

"You know I wouldn't miss one of your parties, Sandy."

Sylvia and Athena changed into their swim suits and joined the others at the pool. Sylvia, wearing a red and white-striped string bikini, and Athena, in a conservative black one-piece suit, had barely sat down before mint juleps—served in silver mugs—were thrust into their hands.

"I haven't had one of these since I attended the

Kentucky Derby last year," Sylvia said. She took a sip from her mug. "It's delicious."

"Mike and Sandy are known for making perfect juleps," Copland informed the group. "Several of us have tried to find out how they make them, but they refuse to tell. We have found one thing out, though. They have a secret recipe that they keep locked in a vault." Everyone laughed and teased their hosts.

Sylvia shifted in her chair and her eyes caught sight of Justin in snow-white, brief swimming trunks, positioned on the diving board. He easily executed a complicated dive before his taut, well-developed body splashed into the water. He glided to the side of the pool and pulled himself out. Applause greeted him, and he acknowledged the appreciation of his efforts with a smile and a quick bow of his head. He took a seat at the far end of the pool and began to slowly drink from his mug. All the while, his eyes were fastened on Sylvia. Boldly, she returned his admiring gaze.

"Is the barbeque ready yet?" someone shouted across the pool to Mike. "I'm starving." The spell was broken; Sylvia's attention snapped back to the party.

"We'll have to give it another thirty, forty minutes," Mike answered.

"Dance instead of thinking about your stomach," someone else yelled, and turned the music louder. As couples began to fill the deck, Sylvia felt a light tap on her shoulder.

"Would you like to dance?" a middle-aged gentleman asked her.

"I'd love to," she replied. She danced with him and several others afterwards. She wanted so very much to dance with Justin, but for some reason he seemed to be avoiding her. Finally, she accepted a male guest's invitation to sit at one of the tables and talk. She realized after she sat down with him, to her dismay, that he had gulped one mint julep too many and was having difficulty keeping his hands to himself. "Please don't" she pleaded, gently pushing his hand off her knee for the third time. He grabbed her and tried to pull her into his lap, but she successfully wriggled out of his grip. He was getting angry, and Sylvia wondered how she was going to get away from him without creating a scene. At that moment, she heard Justin call the young man, Tim, by name, in a low, controlled voice. And before she could focus clearly, Justin had picked Tim up and thrown him into the pool. Tim floundered about briefly before he made his way to the side of the pool where he stood looking confused.

"Nice going," Mike congratulated Justin thinking he and Tim were kidding around.

"Thanks," Justin responded drily. He took Sylvia by the hand and led her to the deck where others were still dancing. Wrapping both his arms arund her waist, he began to move to the beat of the music. Justin held her so closely, she had no choice but to rest her head against his chest and enfold him in her arms. She listened contentedly to the rapid beating of his heart, luxuriating in the feel of his lean, hard body pressing against hers, as she inhaled deeply the sweet smell of him. When the music ended, he pulled away from her slowly, their bodies peeling apart like tape from a spool.

"Think you can stay out of trouble?" he asked, holding her at arms length.

"Sure," she answered flippantly. But her heart beat was erratic and she felt a little shaky. His eyes lingered on her for a moment before he dropped his hands and walked away.

"May I have a glass of water, please," she asked a passing waiter. He brought her a tall glass filled with water and ice, and Sylvia found a chair and sat down to drink it.

"Are you enjoying yourself?" Athena asked, sitting down beside her.

"Very much.

"I'm glad." Before Athena could say more, another guest called her to join him at table tennis and again Sylvia was left alone.

"Howdy." Sylvia almost spilled her water trying to remove the big, soft, clammy hand caressing her left shoulder. "You're a pretty little thing." A short, fat, balding man stood over her grinning like a Chesire cat.

"It's time to go," Justin said, appearing out of nowhere. He took Sylvia by the hand and walked over to where Sandy and Athena were standing. "Sylvia's not feeling well and I'm taking her home."

Athena looked surprised. "You should have told me you weren't feeling well," she said.

"It's just a little headache," Sylvia lied. "I'll take something for it and get to bed early. I'm sure I'll feel better in the morning."

"I hope so," Athena said, looking at her worriedly.

Sylvia couldn't believe how quickly the false words had slipped through her lips. Why am I going along with Justin's lie? she asked herself. Why am I allowing him to order me about? Although it was a relief to get away from her obnoxious admirers, she wasn't sure she should be leaving the party with Justin. Was he sincerely concerned about her welfare or was this just a ruse to get her back to the ranch alone? He sure had a big surprise coming if he thought for a minute she would be foolish enough to be his toy for the night. She would have no part of Justin Udall's amorous advances.

With their totes slung over their shoulders, Justin and Sylvia said goodbye to the other guests and walked away toward the road.

"Aren't you taking the car?" Athena called after them.

"No, the walk will be good for Sylvia's headache," Justin replied.

"But it's two miles, Justin."

"The longer the walk, the better it is for her headache."

Athena watched them walk away, shaking her head in resignation.

They walked along the narrow paved road, which was bordered on both sides by thick woods. Sylvia could hear an occasional rustle in the underbrush as they moved along and knew wildcats or wolves were probably nearby.

"Your sister thinks you're crazy," she said, stealing a glance at Justin.

"Correction," he countered. "You think I'm crazy."

"So true."

Justin laughed softly.

"You heard me?" she asked. She had not intended for him to hear her words.

"I heard you," he said, giving her a sidelong look.

She wondered what Justin was like when he was irritated before remembering she already knew. "Angry?"

"Do I look angry?"

"No."

"Your question is answered."

"I'm glad I didn't hurt your feelings." She wasn't in the mood for Justin to give her the cold shoulder, especially not along this long, desolate road.

"You didn't hurt my feelings, Lovely Lady," he said, flashing his hypnotic smile.

"I did yesterday," she said, seizing the opportunity to find out why he didn't seem to like the idea of her selling his work at Emary Oaks.

"I don't know what you mean." It was twilight and Sylvia moved closer to him in the approaching darkness.

"I mean you were angry yesterday because I bought more of your art from Athena." She looked up at him expecting an answer, but he remained silent. They walked in silence for about a quarter of a mile. She had hoped that since he was in an agreeable mood she could talk with him about purchasing his work, but obviously she was wrong. They had reached their usual impasse. For some strange reason, Justin seemed opposed to her buying his work and she intended to find out why. "Did you hear me?" she finally asked, leaning so close to him that they bumped into each other.

"I heard you," he said. "We're almost home. Tired?"

"No. Lonely."

He chuckled. "You have a wonderful sense of humor."

"You have a wonderful way of avoiding the issue."

"Yes, I ignore it."

"And quite blatantly."

They walked the remainder of the trip without conversation. When they arrived at the house, Justin led

Sylvia around the side to the pool.

"Hungry?" he asked.

"Yes."

"Would you like to help me fix something for us to eat?"

"No," Sylvia responded, flopping down in one of the lounge chairs.

"Mmmm. The lovely lady has a mean streak. What would you like?"

He stood over her—still clad only in the brief white swimming trunks—with both hands on his hips. The sight of him in such an alluring pose sent short waves of chills up and down Sylvia's spine. She wondered if Polly Vance was close to acquiring papers of ownership on this object d'art.

"A few slices of that cow your neighbors had on the grill would be nice," she said.

"You forfeited your barbecued beef dinner by not staying out of trouble." He sat down on the edge of her chair.

"I usually handle those types of situations much better than I did today."

"I'm sure," he said, his attention drawn to her scantily-clad body. "Maybe next time you should try covering up a little more of what tends to make a man lose his head."

She grew uncomfortable under his gaze and with his comment. She had realized earlier that her swim suit was much too brief for the occasion. "I'm sure you're right," she agreed quickly. "Now, back to dinner."

"Yes. Please." His face broke into a smile.

"A sandwich will do."

"Good. I'm an expert at making sandwiches." He got

up and walked away.

Sylvia relaxed on the lounge chair, staring out in the distance. She wondered why Justin acted so strangely each time she mentioned buying his art. There was a problem and she hoped they would get it resolved soon. She didn't want anyone to beat her to exclusive rights to sell his art in Houston.

It wasn't long before Justin was back at her side with a tray of sandwiches and a bottle of wine in an ice bucket. "Miss me?" he asked.

"No."

He laughed softly. "Don't be so mean, Lovely Lady," he said.

"What do we have here?" she asked, sitting up. "Looks good," she said, picking up one of the sandwiches and taking a bite out of it. "Mmmm, it is good."

"I'm glad you like it. I hope it hits the spot."

"It will."

Their banter ceased and they ate in silence. But they both felt the magnetism that kept drawing their eyes to each other. Too often, Sylvia's heart beat spasmodically as her gaze involuntarily met Justin's. Tension between them mounted, and she hurriedly finished her sandwich. Her emotions frightened her. After all, she was supposed to be planning her marriage to Armand. "Thanks for playing bodyguard and for dinner," she said, getting up from the chair. "I think I'll go to my room now."

"Not yet," Justin said, catching her hand before she could get out of his reach. His voice was gentle, but commanding. They stood gazing at each other for a second before he drew her to him and began kissing her passionately. Sylvia, gathering all of her strength—for that's what it took for her to resist Justin—planted both hands firmly against his naked, muscular chest and pushed him away from her.

For a moment he stared at her, and then an amused expression crawled across his handsome face. "Not so easy this time, huh?" he spoke teasingly.

Sylvia, stunned by his cruel words, fought back hot tears that immediately sprang to her eyes. When her mind began to function more clearly, the numbness that had momentarily overtaken her was replaced with fury. She lunged at Justin, caught him off balance, and he tumbled into the pool. She spun on her heels and ran toward the house. Within seconds, Justin pulled himself out of the water and ran after her.

He managed to overtake her just as she was about to enter the side door. Gently, he grasped her by the shoulders and turned her to face him. "I'm sorry," he said. "That was totally unnecessary and unfair. Please forgive me, Sylvia."

Rigid with anger, her large dark eyes studied him closely. Sincerity was written on his face, and she realized he had not really meant to hurt her. Gradually, her anger began to subside. She pulled away from him and walked to the pool. A lazy breeze stirred and she welcomed the cooling effect it had on her skin.

"Am I forgiven?" Justin asked, coming over to face her.

"Yes," she said, avoiding his gaze.

"Thank you." His voice was low and husky as he took both her hands in his own. "I'm really sorry," he said. Slowly he brought her hands to his lips, turned the palms up and gently covered them with kisses. Sylvia's breath caught in her throat. Justin's gentle besiegement progressed to her shoulders and neck. Impassioned, she sagged against him and he clasped her to his body. His mouth covered hers with a lingering kiss, while his hands began to leisurely caress her torso.

"Justin, please stop." She breathlessly forced the words through her lips.

Reluctantly, he tore his body from hers and stood looking at her intently. "You're a beautiful and desirable woman, Sylvia," he said.

Her legs were shaking, but she managed to pick up her tote bag and head for the house. "Goodnight, Justin," she said. "Sleep well." She could feel his eyes on her as she walked away.

"Goodnight, Lovely Lady," she heard him say softly. When she reached the door, she paused before opening it and watched him dive into the pool and swim its length.

After lunch on Sunday, Justin drove Sylvia to the airport. They had left the ranch late and arrived with just enough time for her to board the plane. Justin kissed her lightly on the lips and handed her a package. "I thought you might like this," he said. "It was custom-made just for you."

Surprised, Sylvia took the package from him and hurried to board her flight. When the plane was airborne, she unwrapped the package and found an exquisite painting of a sun setting over a stretch of grassland. So that's what Justin had been doing when she wondered about him on Saturday, she thought. Her eyes filled with tears. Justin was a difficult, arrogant man, but he was also capable of deep kindness and thought-fulness. Carefully she rewrapped the painting. She knew she would treasure it always.

Chapter Four

Sylvia spent the next several days traveling around the state shopping for native arts and crafts for the store. She was fortunate in finding intricately-designed hand-made quilts in Waco and antique pottery in Huntsville. Her most exciting find, however, had been in Lufkin. The blacksmith's work that Paul had told her about was both unique and elegant. Perfect items for the Nook of International Treasures. She would always be indebted to Paul for sharing his excellent sources. Her new buys and Justin's camvases were sure to make her Christmas project a smashing success.

With the approaching holidays, Sylvia's work in the office had become progressively demanding. New shipments were coming in almost every day. She was constantly busy at her desk, as well as in the Nook of International Treasures where she changed merchandise around in order to make room for new stock. She was examining a shipment that had arrived from Tunisia when Henrika, flushed with excitement, joined her in the office.

"I thought you'd like to know that the shop made more money during the week we carried the Udall paintings than any other week of its history," she announced.

"So what else is new?" Sylvia asked smugly.

"Oh, don't be so arrogant," Henrika said, perching on top of her desk. "When is the new shipment due? I'm anxious to see if it will sell as well as the first one."

Sylvia began clearing her desk of all the papers and other articles that were strewn over its surface. "Athena called last week to say that it would take her longer than she had anticipated to get the canvases packed properly and shipped. But I'm expecting them any day now. You're just going to adore the pieces I chose this time, Henrika."

"I know I will," Henrika said, walking over to Sylvia and giving her a hug and a kiss. "I just hope I don't buy them all before we can get them on the floor." She laughed at herself as she crossed the room to the office door. "By the way," she said, pausing for a second, "you're in for a big Christmas bonus." She winked a sparkling green eye at Sylvia and left the office.

Sylvia finished clearing her desk and left Emary Oaks for the Galleria Shopping Center where she had agreed to meet Bluma for lunch. Her busy schedule had prevented her from talking with her friend during the past week and a half, and she looked forward to seeing her.

"Have you been waiting long?" she asked, greeting Bluma in front of the Magic Pan Restaurant.

"Only a couple of minutes." The restaurant was crowded when they got inside and they had to wait fifteen minutes for a table. But as soon as they were seated, the waitress took their order. Within a short period of time, they were enjoying the hot, tasty crepes for which the restaurant was noted.

"I hate admitting this, Bluma," Sylvia said, "but you were right."

"About what?" Her friend looked at her in surprise.

"Justin. I like him a lot."

"Who is Justin?" Mr. Fantastic Artist?"

"What a short memory you have, my dear," Sylvia said sarcastically. "Yes." She told Bluma all about her weekend on the Udall ranch.

"So what are you going to do about Armand?"

"What do you mean?"

"You should break your engagement, Sylvia."

"But I'm not in love with Justin," she argued. "I just like him a lot."

"Are you in love with Armand?"

She had never been asked that question directly before, not by Armand nor anyone else. Bluma had an awful lot of nerve.

"What do you mean?" she asked, feeling perspiration form on her brow and upper lip. Her tone was arrogant and she realized the question had made her feel defensive.

"It was a simple question, Sylvia. Do you love Armand?"

Bluma was overstepping her bounds and it angered her. Even close friends should recognize when they were getting too personal. "Would I make plans to marry him if I didn't?" Her words rushed out in a hiss and her heart began to thump in her chest.

"Be fair to yourself and Armand," Bluma said in a soft voice. "Answer the question."

Why did Bluma always think she was so right? Sylvia thought. It was really none of her business whether or not she loved Armand. What did it matter to her? Why was she pressing the issue? She nervously sipped from her glass of ice water. Did she love Armand? That was a question she had never asked herself. Why did she have to answer it now? Because it was fair? She dabbed her mouth with her napkin. Yes, it was a fair question and it deserved a fair answer.

"I'm not sure," she whispered.

"Then I think you should give the question some serious thought," Bluma said, "and soon."

Sylvia drove back to work preoccupied with the conversation she'd had with Bluma. When she first spoke the words that had answered Bluma's question, she had known they weren't true. No, she said to herself as she drove through the heavy lunch hour traffic. I don't love Armand Brandon. It had been difficult, but she had at last answered the question honestly to herself. A feeling of relief rushed through her body, but at the same time a strong feeling of sadness gripped her. She would have to tell Armand that she could not be his wife. That would be hard. She didn't relish the idea of hurting him. How had it happened? Frankly, it had been easy. Armand had assumed she would marry him and she had gone along with his assumption because, at the time, she had decided he was right for her. The frightening thing was she had almost convinced herself that she was doing the right thing. Thanks to Bluma she had finally faced the issue. She felt guilty for allowing Armand to think for so long that she would marry him, and realized she should have put an end to it months ago. She had been completely out of character. It was not her style to allow others' assumptions or desires to rule her life, particularly about something as important as marriage. She would have to tell Armand immediately that she could not be his wife.

*   *   *

Sylvia had been trying to shut off her alarm clock for several seconds before she realized it was the telephone that was jarring her nerves.

"You were asleep?" The familiar deep voice brought her to full consciousness. Her heart beat increased and her temperature felt like it had shot up ten degrees.

"No...no. Not really," she stammered.

"Mmmm. What does that mean? You're in bed, but not alone?"

"Of course I'm alone, Justin," she said coolly. "Where are you?"

"The Warwick Hotel."

"In Houston?" She struggled to keep her excitement under control.

"Yep. What are you doing asleep at this time of night, Lovely Lady? It's only nine-thirty."

"I must have dozed off," Sylvia said. "I'm supposed to be watching TV."

"Boring program?"

"No. Rough day at the store."

"I see." After exchanging information about the welfare of their families and work, Justin informed Sylvia he had come to Houston for the Starving Artists Art Show. Two of his former students were showing their work and he wanted to give them moral support. He would be in the city for a couple of days and wanted to know if he could take her to dinner the following night. Sylvia accepted his invitation.

The next morning at work, Sylvia excitedly told Henrika that Justin was in town and she was to have dinner with him that night.

"That's terrific," Henrika said, her excitement matching Sylvia's.

"I think I'll leave the store a couple of hours early to get ready for my big date."

"It's fine with me," Henrika told her. "Take all the time you need, and by all means please invite Mr. Udall to come to the store tomorrow." Sylvia promised she would.

After enjoying a warm bubble bath and washing and drying her hair, Sylvia dressed for her night out with Justin. She pulled her tomato-red silk jersey dress, with tiered skirt and one-shouldered bodice, over her head, feeling that it suited her happy mood. She completed her outfit with high-heeled red satin sandals and a small green silk handbag. With deliberation, she dabbed her favorite perfume at the pressure points of her body and slipped pearl stud earrings into her ears.

Justin picked her up at seven and they went to an intimate little restaurant. Dinner was enjoyable, and for a while the evening progressed perfectly.

"What's wrong with your eyes?" Sylvia asked. Justin's eyes were tearing and red. He had continuously wiped them with a tissue throughout dinner.

"Nothing," he answered.

"They look awful," Sylvia persisted. "Do they hurt?"

"Thanks for the kind compliment," Justin said tightly, "and no, they don't hurt."

"I wasn't attempting to compliment you, Justin. I'm just a little worried about your eyes."

"They're all right," he said adamantly.

Although she realized she had annoyed him by asking about his eyes, Sylvia dared to venture further into unsafe waters.

"Your paintings that I bought the week before last finally arrived today," she said, "and Henrika and I would be honored if you'd come to the store tomorrow for a couple of hours to talk with our customers about your work." She studied his face before continuing with caution. "We'd also like to talk with you about exclusive rights to sell your works here in Houston."

"Is that the reason for all the phony concern about my eyes?" His voice was low and angry.

"My concern for your eyes is quite genuine, Justin," Sylvia said. "However, the fact remains that we'd like you to come to the store tomorrow and we'd like exclusive rights to sell your work here in the city."

A cynical smile tugged at Justin's lips. "I never intend to sell to you or anyone else at Emary Oaks again." His tone was cold.

Although she had anticipated an argument, she was totally unprepared for his unequivocal refusal. "But why, Justin?" Sylvia asked.

"I have my reasons," he answered, "and I don't intend to discuss them now."

"We've done so well with your work," she persisted, still in shock. "Why wouldn't you want us to handle you?"

"I've made my decision," he said impassively.

"And it's an awfully stupid one," she informed him.

"You're entitled to your opinon." He helped her out of her chair, and they made their way to the parking lot and back to her condominium.

"Goodnight, Justin," she said turning to him once she

had opened the door. "Thanks for dinner."

Deliberately, he leaned against the door frame preventing her from closing the door. "You're not inviting me in for coffee, tea or milk?" he asked, allowing a smile to slowly creep across his face.

"I thought maybe you had better things to do," she answered dully.

"There's nothing I'd rather do with my time tonight than spend it with you, Lovely Lady," he said, walking past her into her living room. "The home reflects the lady's elegant taste," he added, looking about. "Charming."

"Thanks," Sylvia said. She threw her purse onto a chair and with exaggeration asked, "Coffee, tea or milk?"

"Tea will be perfect."

She went to the kitchen and he began a slow inspection of a wall that she had covered from ceiling to floor with small paintings and other objects of art. "A couple of these paintings are really excellent," he said over his shoulder. "Who's the artist?"

"Which ones are you talking about?" Sylvia asked, poking her head out of the kitchen door.

"The sunset and the wild flowers."

"Oh, yes," she said, returning to her work in the kitchen. "The artist is some weird guy in Dallas. As you can see, he's a fantastic talent, but personally I question his mental health."

Justin laughed good-naturedly. "Give the poor guy a break. By the way, I accept your invitation to come to the store tomorrow."

Sylvia almost dropped the delicate china cup and saucer that she had in her hands. "Good," she said. She walked out of the kitchen and stood next to him.

"What time?"

"One o'clock should be okay."

"I'll be there." He moved away from her down the wall. "I really like your collection," he said, examining a dark wood carving of a man's head. "Where did this come from?"

"Africa. Nigeria."

"And this one?" He pointed to a sleek figure carved of teakwood.

"Denmark."

"Copenhagen?"

"Yes."

"Your work has taken you to many interesting places," he observed.

"Yes. I've been fortunate. Did you see this?" she asked, reaching across him and picking up a small, elaborately-carved mask.

"No. Tell me about it." He took a lock of her hair between his fingers and brought it to his nose. After inhaling deeply, he emitted a low, passionate moan. "I like the way it smells," he said, smiling and running his fingers through her hair.

Sylvia turned to look at him and their eyes locked. She tried to turn away, but Justin gently took her face in both his hands and brought it closer to his own. Her breath caught in her throat and she could feel herself submitting to his will. "This is from Africa, also," she said. Her speech was labored.

"This is too," Justin countered, moving his face even closer to hers. "Via the U.S. of A." He kissed the tip of her nose lightly. "And to be more specific," he kissed both her eyelids, "these kisses come to you straight from Dallas." They both giggled and Sylvia took the opportunity to pull away from him and change the subject.

"I'm still worried about your eyes, Justin," she said. "Are you sure they don't hurt?"

"They're beginning to sting a little, but they'll be all right." He reached for her and willingly she went to him. "I didn't imagine it," he whispered. "It really is wonderful holding you." His hands roamed over her body, leaving a trail of pleasure in their wake. A soft cry of passion slipped through Sylvia's lips and she pressed her body, aching with desire, hard against him. With one hand holding her tightly in place, he slipped his free hand in her hair and tenderly pulled her head from his chest. His eyes raked her face and neck. "You're so very, very lovely," he groaned before devouring her lips with hungry, probing kisses. Sylvia allowed herself to bask in the warm tenderness of Justin's affection before reluctantly extricating herself from his embrace. "I think the tea has steeped long enough," she said breathlessly. She went to the kitchen and brought out a tray set with tea for two. They chatted amiably as they sipped their tea, and Justin left shortly afterwards.

Sylvia unpacked and priced Justin's paintings as soon as she arrived at the store the next day. She decided to display them in groups of five, leaving the others stacked against the wall for customers to go through if they desired. The first five had been chosen when Henrika came into the office.

"Justin promised to be here at one o'clock today,"

Sylvia announced.

"Oh, you did it!" Henrika was excited. "Thank you, Sylvia." She walked over to the new canvases and began looking through them.

"Not again," Sylvia said, watching her.

"Yes, again." Henrika leisurely inspected each canvas before turning and smiling broadly at Sylvia.

"How many this time?"

Henrika held up three fingers. "I'm controlling myself," she declared.

Sylvia took the remaining paintings out and arranged them in the Nook of International Treasures. Pleased with her displays, she returned to her work in the office. Before one o'clock, three of the canvases had been sold.

At five minutes after one, Mary burst into the office in a flustered state. "There's a man out in the shop asking for you, Sylvia. He is really, really good looking." She nervously arranged her hair and adjusted her skirt.

"That would be Mr. Udall," Sylvia said, getting up from her desk casually. "Tell him I'll be right out." Her heart began to pound in her chest, and she had to take a couple of deep breaths to compose herself.

When she reached the shop, Henrika and Justin had introduced themselves and were deep in conversation. Sylvia paused for a moment and observed them. Justin was strikingly handsome in a white tailor-made safari suit and dark brown leather cowboy boots. As she approached them, she wondered if he owned a pair of regular shoes.

"Hello, Justin. I see you've met the owner of the Nook of International Treasures."

"At long last," Henrika said. "Thanks again, Justin,

for accepting our invitation."

"It's a pleasure to be here," Justin responded. They chatted for several minutes before Henrika seized the opportunity to tell Justin how very much she liked his work and how honored she would be if he allowed her to handle him exclusively in Houston. Before Justin or Sylvia could respond to her statement, the small shop began to fill with customers. Happily, Henrika introduced Justin and his canvases to them. Mary and another saleswoman, Cathy, circulated around the room serving wine in long-stemmed glasses while Justin talked about his art and himself. He was gracious and charming, and the customers, as well as the saleswomen and Henrika, were fascinated by him. He stayed at the shop for a couple of hours. It pleased Sylvia that during that time, six of his paintings were sold. She worried about him, however, because his eyes seemed even more inflamed than the day before. But she didn't dare question him about them. He left the store after kissing both Sylvia and Henrika lightly on the cheeks.

Sylvia walked with Henrika back to the office, feeling letdown because Justin did not mention seeing her again before going back to Dallas. She sat slumped over her desk, staring out the window.

"Is anything wrong?" Henrika asked, noticing Sylvia's despondent gaze.

"I might as well tell you now, Henrika," she said, not addressing the major reason for her unhappiness. "Justin told me last night at dinner that he never intends to sell to us again."

"Surely he was only teasing," Henrika replied. "He seemed awfully pleased today with how we are handling his work."

"He was dead serious," Sylvia insisted.

Henrika looked confused. "Then please do whatever it takes, Sylvia, to get him to change his mind. Obviously, he is going to make it big soon, and I want Emary Oaks to be a part of that success."

Sylvia turned on Henrika angrily. "I won't sell my soul to the devil for a few lousy paintings, Henrika." Her voice was husky and emotional.

"I didn't realize you'd have to, Sylvia," Henrika replied, startled by her friend's sharp tone. "Do what you can. I'd appreciate it." She started out the door and hesitated. "I think it's terrific that you're in love with Justin, Sylvia. He's really a fantastic guy." She left the office, closing the door softly behind her, while Sylvia sat with her mouth open.

Henrika's parting words were infuriating, but Sylvia knew they were true. She was in love with Justin Udall.

Sylvia was strumming her guitar and singing when the telephone interrupted her solitary performance. It was Justin, and his voice indicated a somber mood.

"I'm sorry to disturb your evening, Sylvia, but my eyes have worsened and I think I'll have to see a doctor. Do you have any recommendations. I suppose I should see an ophthalmologist."

Sylvia glanced at her clock. "It's after six, Justin. I'm sure most doctors have closed their offices for the night. You'll probably have to go to the emergency ward in the Medical Center."

"I hadn't thought of that," he said dully. "Thanks, Sylvia. That's what I'll do."

"Justin?"

"Yes?"

"Would you like me to drive you?"

"That won't be necessary," he said. "I can get a cab."

"If that's what you prefer," she replied. "But I thought perhaps you'd like someone to hold your hand while you wait to see the doctor."

"Are you suggesting the cab driver won't do that?" His tone had not changed.

"Yes," she said, laughing softly.

"See you in twenty minutes," he said, and hung up the phone.

Hurriedly, Sylvia changed into a pair of white slacks and a white shirt, and drove to the Warwick Hotel. Justin was waiting for her out front. He slid into the passenger seat, and Sylvia headed for the Medical Center.

"I'm glad I didn't go blind before seeing this," he said. "Where did you find such a magnificent car?"

"Please don't say things like that about your eyes," she implored. "I'm sure nothing is seriously wrong with them."

"Don't sound so grim, Lovely Lady. I'll be able to behold your exquisite beauty for the next hundred years. Now, tell me about the car."

"My uncle gave it to me when I graduated from college," she said.

"Your uncle has excellent taste." He rested his head against the back of the seat and closed his eyes. Sylvia gave him a long, penetrating glance. "Go on and say it and get it over with."

"Say what?"

He turned his head so that he could look at her. "That

I should have seen a doctor before now. But I thought the drops I was using would clear them up. I had no idea they would get worse. Besides," he smiled self-consciously, "I don't like doctors."

"I wasn't going to say anything to you about what you should have done," Sylvia informed him. "I'm just glad you've finally decided to have your eyes examined."

She parked in the hospital parking lot and they walked hand in hand to the emergency room. After they had waited for half an hour, the doctor examined Justin's eyes and informed him that he had an eye infection caused by pollen and pollution. He was given a prescription and advised to remain indoors and not use his eyes for forty-eight hours.

Justin related the doctor's diagnosis and advice to Sylvia. She could tell that he was unnerved by the information. However, it was a relief to know that he was not seriously ill. He would not be able to drive back to Dallas on schedule.

They stopped at a pharmacy and had his prescription filled, then drove back to the hotel. All the while, Sylvia felt an obligation to invite Justin to spend the next two days with her since he was all alone in the city and was not well. Also, she could not forget that she had been a guest in his home, and common courtesy dictated that she should at least offer the invitation. She was sure he would not accept, since they both realized that being together in such close quarters would surely create a volatile situation. She pulled in front of the hotel and parked.

"Would you like to spend the next two days with me, Justin?" she asked. "You're welcome to my sofabed."

For the first time since they left the hospital, Justin's

face lit up with a smile and he spoke without hesitation. "I'd hate to spend two days alone in a hotel room, unable to paint, read or even watch TV," he said. "Thanks, Sylvia. I'll get my things." He got out of the car and disappeared through the double doors of the hotel.

Shocked, Sylvia sat in her car gripping the steering wheel, realizing she had made a terrible mistake. Justin checked out of his room and made arrangements to leave his car in the hotel garage until Sunday evening. Sylvia then drove them to her condominium.

She showed Justin where to hang his clothes and wash up, and then prepared a light dinner, which they ate by candlelight.

"Now what am I supposed to do?" he asked her, as she tidied up the kitchen.

She had been wondering the same thing. She wasn't sleepy and she knew he wasn't either. "Take your medication," she said, handing him a glass of water and a small bottle. He swallowed the capsule that the doctor had prescribed and handed the glass back to her.

"Now what?"

Sylvia walked out of the kitchen into the living room, with Justin close on her heels. Her eyes caught sight of An Anthology of Verse by American Negroes, on her bookshelf. "Sit down," she said picking up the book. "I'll read to you." She was thankful that she had finally thought of some way to entertain him.

"Oh, goody," he said wryly.

She settled herself on the sofa next to him and opened the book. "In this anthology there are poems that are serious and poems that are not serious," she announced. "Which would you like to hear?"

"The ones that are in-between," he answered with a straight face, and moved closer to her.

She laughed in spite of herself. "Don't get too close," she warned him. "The light may hurt your eyes."

"I'll keep them shut. Read." He took one of her hands in his, put his feet up on the ottoman in front of him, and rested his head on the back of the sofa. "Ready," he said.

Sylvia read several poems by Paul Laurence Dunbar and James Weldon Johnson. "Bored?" she asked after twenty minutes.

"Not at all," he answered, shaking his head vigorously. "I love those poems. Most of them I've never heard before." He opened his eyes and looked at her. "And I especially like your voice. Everything is perfect." He readjusted his grip on her hand. "More," he commanded.

Sylvia continued to read, choosing from the works of Countee Cullen, Georgia Douglas Johnson, Claude McKay and several others. "Your medication is putting you to sleep," she finally said, looking over at him. "Change into your pajamas and I'll make your bed."

Obediently, Justin followed Sylvia's instructions. When he returned to the living room, his bed was ready and he crawled in and stretched out. "Afraid, Sylvia?" he asked.

"Of you, Justin?" She knew the medication would have him asleep within minutes.

"No," he said, shaking his head. His hypnotic smile pulled at one corner of his lips. "Of yourself."

Sylvia laughed heartily. "Not to worry, Justin," she cooed. "I've never attacked a diseased, doped-up man before, and I doubt seriously if I will tonight."

Justin laughed into his pillow. "Don't I even get a goodnight kiss?" he persisted groggily.

"Perhaps I'll consider it when you're germ free," she said flippantly. Before she could get out of the room and close the door behind her, he was sound asleep.

The next morning they both slept late. Sylvia prepared breakfast for Justin and joined him at the table for a cup of tea. Armand was picking her up within the hour for an early lunch.

"I'll have to leave you for a few hours this afternoon," she said. "But I'm sure you can find something to do with your time."

"Henrika has you working today?"

"No," she acknowledged. "I have a lunch date with a friend."

"Why can't she have lunch with you here?" he asked. "Am I so terrible you don't want anyone to see me?" She knew he was only teasing, and she hated to tell him the truth.

"My lunch date is not a she," she said distinctly. "He is a he. And we have something rather private to discuss." She got up from the table and started to the bedroom to get dressed.

"I think you're being very rude, Sylvia," he told her. He was annoyed, as she knew he would be. But she couldn't cancel with Armand. She had to tell him today that she could never be his wife. "After all," Justin continued, "I am your guest. Your first obligation is to me." He followed her to the door and yelled through it. "Not only am I a guest in your home, I am also disabled."

"I know," she yelled back. "But I noticed your eyes this morning. They look much better."

"What'll I do here all by myself?"

She opened the door dressed in an aqua and navy cotton suit and navy high-heeled leather sandals. "Here," she said, thrusting her guitar into his hands. "You're a cowboy. Pretend you're on the lonesome trail."

There was a light rapping on the door and she went to open it for Armand. He came in and Sylvia introduced the two men.

"Justin is the artist who painted these two canvases," she said, pointing to Justin's work on her wall.

"Oh yes," Armand replied, "your art is pretty nice, man. And congratulations on your success at Emary Oaks. I understand your work is selling very well."

Justin and Sylvia exchanged glances. "Thanks." Justin scrutinized Armand as he lounged on the sofa with his arms folded across his chest.

"What are you doing in Houston?" Armand asked.

"Business," Justin replied sharply.

"I see."

Sylvia, realizing it was time she intervened, turned to Armand and smiled. "Justin contracted an eye infection since he's been here and can't use his eyes for a couple of days," she explained. "I invited him to come here so he wouldn't have to remain in his hotel room with nothing to do and no one to talk to."

"I'm sorry to hear that," Armand said. "I hope your eyes are better soon." He escorted Sylvia toward the door.

Justin got up from the sofa and followed them. "I'm sure you do," he replied sardonically.

Sylvia knew Justin had assumed Armand was displeased with him being in her home, but she knew better. Armand was sincere in wishing Justin good health. He was a very trusting and kind man. "We'll see you later," she said, with a little wave.

"Goodbye," Justin replied lightheartedly. "And by the way, Armand," he stuck his head out the door. "Sylvia has to be in by four." Solemnly, he shut the door in their blank faces.

Sylvia was extremely nervous all through lunch, but Armand didn't seem to notice. He had busied himself with telling her about a new project he had initiated in his company. They were having coffee when she broached the subject of their marriage.

"Armand," she spoke softly, "I've given our relationship a lot of thought lately and I've come to realize it would be an awful mistake for us to marry." Her heart ached as she watched him.

"Why, Sylvia?" A frown wrinkled his brow and he looked at her, disbelieving what she had just said to him.

Although it was difficult, she knew she had to go on. "I like you very much," she said, "but I don't love you."

"You can't mean that." His voice was barely audible. "Have you found someone that you do love?" He squeezed his eyes shut and tightened his jaw. There was a long silence.

"No," she lied.

His eyes searched her face. "Is it Justin?" She could detect anger growing in his voice.

"No," she said quickly. Her heart had skipped a beat at the sound of Justin's name, but she persisted in her lie.

"I love you very much, Sylvia."

"I know."

His speech was labored. "If there is no one else, I'd like to continue seeing you."

"Of course, Armand," she said. "I'll always consider you a very dear friend."

"Maybe you'll change your mind again." His voice had grown a bit stronger, his speech clearer.

Watching him, Sylvia realized Armand was desperately hoping her decision to break their engagement was just a passing fancy. "No, Armand," she said gently. "I won't change my mind."

With nothing more to say, they left the restaurant.

Emotionally drained, Sylvia let herself in through the front door.

"Is that a burglar?" Justin called out.

"It's me, Justin," she said. She walked into the living room and was surprised to see him sitting on the sofa strumming her guitar. She sat across from him on a chair.

"How was lunch?"

"Fine."

"You don't look like lunch was fine."

"Armand and I had a very serious talk," she sighed. "The subject wasn't very pleasant. But I'm all right."

"Would you like to talk about it?"

"No. Not now," she said, shaking her head.

"All right. But whether you like it or not, you're going to be serenaded this minute." He struck a loud chord on the guitar. "Ditty Number One," he announced.

"Justin," Sylvia interrupted him. "Haven't you forgotten something very important?" She kicked her shoes off and folded her legs under her.

"What's that?" he asked, still strumming the guitar softly.

"You can't sing."

"Oh, yes." He laughed good-humoredly. "But you will be happy to know that during my performance you will be so taken by the fact that I also cannot play the guitar, you won't even notice I can't sing."

Sylvia laughed. "I feel better already," she said.

He began playing a tune with a bluesy beat. It was obvious that Justin was skilled at playing the instrument. With an exaggerated southern accent, he half-talked and half-sang about Sylvia's physical beauty, pointing out his appreciation for her height, figure, hair, eyes and complexion. It was a rhythmic little song, and Sylvia burst into applause when he had finished.

"Oh, thank you, Justin," she said. "That was very cute."

"It's only the beginning," he told her, running his fingers lightly over the strings of the guitar. "Prepare yourself for Ditty Number Two." To a jazzy little tune he sang about Sylvia's wit, intelligence and charm.

"I can't believe this," Sylvia said, thoroughly enjoying the adulation from Justin. "Did you really make those up while I was out?"

"Yes," he confessed with pretended modesty. "I made them up all by myself. No fairy godmother came to help me. Now, don't move. There's more. This is my favorite. It's called `Lovely Lady'."

The title sent a shiver racing down Sylvia's spine. He began a slow, melodic tune on the guitar, and softly he sang about the happiness of the man who would be fortunate enough to win her as his bride. Sylvia's heart beat quickened as she listened to the words of 'Lovely Lady'. Why had Justin chosen to sing about her as a bride? Was it a deliberate tease? What were his motives? Was he also singing about himself? Was he the fortunate man? She closed her eyes for a moment as she visualized scenes from the song. Dressed in Aunt Bea's wedding gown, she walked down the aisle of one of the largest churches in Houston, which was packed with relatives and friends. Justin was waiting for her at the altar. He took her from her father's arm, and together they went to stand in front of the minister. As they began to repeat their vows, she quickly returned to reality and opened her eyes. She looked at Justin and realized, all during his singing, he had never taken his eyes from her. The song was beautiful, and it was some time before Sylvia could speak again.

"Those were beautiful, Justin," she finally said. "Your many talents surprise me."

"I surprise myself, sometimes," he acknowledged arrogantly. "You're supposed to be cheered up, now." His intense gaze made her uncomfortable, and she shifted in her chair.

"Oh, I am," she said. Her emotions were running the gamut. One minute she was remembering the pain in Armand's gentle face and feeling guilty and depressed. The next, she was exalted by the lyrics of Justin's songs. She tried to sustain an air of gaiety and realized she was not deceiving him or herself. She abandoned her efforts.

"Music is good medicine for the soul," he said casually. "Why don't we listen to some of your favorite tapes."

Sylvia was glad for the suggestion, and chose several

tapes that she thought they both would enjoy. She made tall glasses of minted iced tea that they sipped from as they relaxed on the floor and listened to the music. Their conversation was light and fluid. She could feel her taut muscles slowly begin to relax. Time slipped by, and they were surprised when the clock struck the eight o'clock hour. Nat 'King' Cole was crooning When I Fall in Love, when Justin suddenly stood up. Leaning over, he took Sylvia's hands in his and pulled her to her feet. In the next instant, she was cuddled in his arms and slowly moving to the music.

Justin's hands slowly and skillfully roved her slender body, as his warm, moist and determined lips repeatedly found hers. His sweet assault sent a raging fire through every inch of her. When the music ended, she slumped against him in ecstasy. Still in a stupor, she gathered her strength and tore away from him and went to her room. It was a long and restless night for both of them.

Chapter Five

It was late Sunday evening when Sylvia and Justin approached Dallas in his midnight blue Mercedes 450SL. She had driven the entire trip after they had both agreed that the four-hour drive from Houston, or any portion of it, would be too taxing on Justin's eyes. He needed the remainder of the day for recuperation.

The trip was difficult for Sylvia. The sexual tension of the previous night had grown steadily throughout the day, and she was anxious to put distance between them. With relief, she observed the signs that indicated they would be in the city within the hour. Her moment of ease was short-lived, however, when Justin asked to be taken to the ranch instead of to his house in Dallas. The additional hour and a half of driving, along with the burden of her secret love for him, had her in a state of nervous exhaustion. When she finally pulled into the long driveway of the rambling house, Justin got out of the car and started for the door, taking their belongings with him.

"Don't take my things," Sylvia said, stopping him in his tracks. "I'm not staying the night."

"What do you mean?" There was an edge to his voice

and a scowl distorted his features.

"I'm taking a hotel room in Dallas," she said.

Justin glared at her before he turned, still holding their bags, and continued walking toward the house. "You'll do no such thing, Sylvia," he declared over his shoulder. "You've been driving for almost six hours and I won't allow you to leave here tonight. I'll take you to the city tomorrow."

Too tired to stand her ground, she followed him into the house. They entered the living room, and Sylvia breathed a sigh of relief when she saw Athena and Copland sitting there. Now she wouldn't have to spend another tempting night alone with Justin.

"I was just about to start worrying about you two," Athena said, looking up from her card game. I've called your house at least a dozen times, Justin."

"We got a late start," he said.

Athena embraced Sylvia and then her brother. "How are your eyes?" she asked.

"They're fine," Justin answered. "Sylvia took very good care of me."

"We can see that she has," Copland observed, as he shook his brother-in-law's hand.

Athena nodded in agreement. "I was delighted when Justin called to say you had invited him to stay with you during his ordeal, Sylvia. It had to be difficult for him not to be able to use his eyes."

"The situation has been difficult for both of us," Justin said. He picked up her bag and started out of the room. "I think Sylvia would like to get some rest now."

"Of course," Athena agreed, "but you must be hungry. Copland and I will prepare a light supper for you."

Sylvia was not in the mood to eat anything, but she

knew any protests she made would be ignored. She followed Justin down the familiar hall to the guest room, where he set her bag down and left without a word. She went to the bathroom and washed her face and hands, dreading having to face Justin again so soon. After combing her hair, she left the room to join Athena in the kitchen.

"Your timing is perfect," Copland said when he saw her. "You'll eat out there." He pointed to a small, glass-enclosed room off the kitchen. The table had been set for two. Candles were flickering in silver candelabras. Justin was already seated at the table. She took the two large chicken salads Copland handed her and went to join him.

"Enjoy your meal, and we'll see you in the morning," Athena said, as she and Copland left the room.

"Thanks for being a good sport," Justin said as she sat down. "I know you could have done without this cozy little dinner."

"I guess we should eat something," she replied, laboriously taking the food into her mouth. "We haven't eaten since midday."

Their conversation remained light and impersonal during the meal. When they had finished, they cleared the table and washed the dishes. Sylvia started out of the kitchen, but Justin stopped her. Taking her face in his hands, he gently drew her to him.

"I haven't thanked you yet for being so kind to me this weekend. I would've been miserable if I had stayed in my hotel room all alone."

"You're very welcome, Justin. It was a pleasure."

Their eyes lingered on each other before Justin's lips claimed hers in a long, smothering kiss. He pressed her compliant body to his, and his deft hands caressed her, spreading the sea of flames within her that only he could ignite or assuage. Their passionate embrace was interrupted by the ringing of the telephone. Justin reached over and picked up the receiver, still holding Sylvia tightly against him. Slowly, his arm fell from her waist.

"I'm much better, Polly," he said.

Knife-like pains pierced Sylvia's heart at the mention of Polly's name. She turned from him and went to her room. She sat on the bed with her legs folded in front of her, her head resting in her hands. Only now did she fully understand the anguish Armand must have experienced on Saturday. What a mess we make of our lives, she thought. Armand was in love with her, but she was in love with Justin, who in turn was in love with Polly. If only it didn't hurt so badly. She got ready for bed, slipped between the sheets, and tried to fall asleep.

The next morning, Sylvia stood on the path between the house and Justin's studio waiting for him. She wanted to tell him goodbye, since she had agreed at breakfast to ride into the city with Athena and Copland. Her plans were to spend the day shopping the markets in Dallas. Later that evening, she would get a flight back to Houston.

Justin came out of the house and walked down the path toward her. "We missed you at breakfast." She attempted to be lighthearted.

"I'll have breakfast in Dallas," he said. "How are you this morning?"

"I'm fine, Justin," she answered. She felt awkward,

but made one last attempt to soften his heart concerning his work. "Since we're standing here," she continued, "I'd like to go to your studio and see your current projects."

"No," Justin said flatly.

She was taken aback by his bluntness. "Why?" she demanded.

"Because it's cruel to let someone see something they may desperately want but will never have." He flashed a smile at her and offered her his arm. "Are you ready to leave for the city now, Miss Random?"

Sylvia ignored his gesture. "Yes, thank you," she answered coolly. "But I will be riding with Athena and Copland." She walked away, and then suddenly stopped and turned to him. "Don't overestimate yourself Justin, and do have a nice day."

"You do the same, Lovely Lady," he said, as he walked to his car, got in and sped away.

The drive into Dallas with Athena and Copland was pleasant. Sylvia congratulated herself for having the foresight to accept their invitation to ride with them. She realized that riding with Justin this morning, in his obviously erratic mood, would only cause her depressed disposition to sink to a lower ebb. She could not suppress her burning desire, however, to find out why he was so inflexible about selling to Emary Oaks.

"Have either of you found out yet why Justin refuses to sell to me?" she asked.

Athena and Copland exchanged glances. The question was allowed to hang in the air for quite some time before Copland decided to speak. "Maybe you should forget about buying Justin's work for a while, Sylvia," he said. He pulled into the campus parking lot of the university where he was a professor of history, and parked the car. "You ladies have a good day." He got out of the car, taking an armload of books and a briefcase with him. "Come back to see us soon, Sylvia," he added. He kissed his wife lightly on the lips and walked away.

"Why don't you ride up front with me," Athena said, sliding under the wheel. Sylvia moved from the back seat to the front, and Athena made her way to the major expressway. "We know why Justin refuses to sell to you, Sylvia, but neither of us agrees with his reasoning. I know I shouldn't interfere, but if you'd like, I'll sell several canvases to you today. I feel so strongly that Emary Oaks could be a tremendous help in launching Justin's career." She pulled in front of the complex where Sylvia planned to begin her shopping for the day. "Why don't you come by the studio after lunch."

"I'd like that, Athena," Sylvia said. "See you then." She got out of the car and made her way up the stairs and through the heavy wooden doors of the building.

Sylvia moved around the room, not really focusing on anything. She browsed through expensive art objects in a detached state for several hours before she decided to leave. Once outside in the midday heat, she resolved to find refuge in one of her favorite restaurants. She hailed a cab and arrived at Richard's minutes before it became crowded with patrons for lunch. She was enjoying a second glass of iced tea and gazing out of the window, when she suddenly sensed someone standing over her. She looked up into Armand's face.

"What are you doing here?" she asked, shocked to see him standing there.

"May I join you?"

"Of course. I'm sorry." She stumbled over her words. "Please sit down, Armand." He sat in the chair across from her. "What are you doing in Dallas?" she asked again.

"As I told you on Saturday," he said, "I'm working on a new project and we're having a three-day conference here in Dallas, starting today."

"Oh, that's wonderful." Sylvia wanted to say something that would ease the pain she saw in his eyes, but could think of nothing. "Have you had lunch?" she asked.

"Yes, with colleagues," he answered. "They've left and I guess I should try to join them before they begin the next meeting." He got to his feet and, simultaneously, they looked toward the entrance of the restaurant in time to see Justin walk in with Polly clinging to his arm. She spotted Sylvia and Armand, and led the way to their table.

"It's been a long time, Sylvia," she cooed. "How are you?"

"Very well, Polly," Sylvia answered coolly. She introduced Polly and Armand.

"I'm happy to see your eyes have improved," Armand said to Justin. His attempt to make light conversation fell on deaf ears. "Thank you," Justin returned sarcastically. "I'm glad to see that your relationship with Sylvia has improved."

Armand looked embarrassed and hurt. "I have to go now, Sylvia," he said. "Perhaps we can have dinner when I get back to Houston."

"I'd love it, Armand," Sylvia replied, trying to make up for Justin's cruel remark. "Please call me." He assured her he would, and walked swiftly out of the restaurant.

Justin watched him go with satisfaction before turning his attention to Sylvia. His eyes raked her unabashedly. She stirred in her chair, growing more and more uneasy under his gaze. Feeling terribly vulnerable, she chided herself for allowing his arrogance to threaten her.

"What time are you leaving Dallas?" he demanded.

"After five," she answered. "Athena is driving me to the airport."

"I see. Athena thinks of everything, doesn't she?"

"She's very kind, Justin."

Lack of attention motivated Polly to take action, and possessively she fastened herself onto Justin's arm. "We'd better find our table, darling," she sang sweetly. "Enjoy your little lunch, Sylvia." They walked away leaving Sylvia with a feeling of weariness.

Feeling that nothing else unpleasant could happen to her, Sylvia left the restaurant and grabbed a cab to the Udall studio. Athena had chosen some canvases that she thought Sylvia would like and had them all arranged on a back wall for her inspection when she arrived. Sylvia chose ten of them, which Athena promised to get in the mail to her the following day. She left the studio to do more shopping, agreeing to return at five o'clock.

Again, Sylvia had trouble working. She gazed at beautiful and elegant objects of art without seeing them. Her fingers moved over a variety of surfaces, unaware of their textures. Her mind had become fixed on Justin and she could not force it to grasp another idea. She found herself wishing time would pass more quickly so that she could get back to Houston. Perhaps there she would be able to move onto other things. Finally, after visiting several showrooms and making two stops for cold drinks, it was time to return to the studio.

She walked in and instantly became aware that something was wrong with Athena. She was tense, and apparently had been crying.

"What happened?" Sylvia was concerned. She sat down across the desk from Athena.

"It's nothing," Athena answered, smiling weakly.

"There has to be something wrong," Sylvia persisted, "or you wouldn't have been crying."

"I must look terrible," she replied. "But don't concern yourself, Sylvia. I'll be all right. I'd better get you to the airport." She got up from her chair and began fumbling through her purse for her keys.

"I'm not leaving here until you tell me why you're so upset," Sylvia pressed. "We're friends, Athena. You can confide in me."

"We're friends, but ..."

"No buts. You'll feel better if you talk about it. I insist."

"All right," Athena said, taking a deep breath and sitting down again in the chair behind the desk. "Since you insist, I guess I have no choice. But please don't let it anger you."

Sylvia looked at her, unblinking. "I'll try," she said.

A long silence permeated the small studio before Athena began to speak. "Justin came by soon after you left this afternoon and we quarreled," she said. "He was very angry that I sold you some of his work, especially since he had asked me not to. Justin and I never fight," Athena continued, "and I guess the fact that we so thoroughly disagree on an issue as important as his work is very upsetting to me."

"I'm sorry I've caused trouble between you and Justin," Sylvia said. "Perhaps we should cancel the purchase."

"No. Not this purchase," Athena objected. "But I will never sell to you again." She fought back tears. "Please try to understand."

"Don't worry," Sylvia said. "I understand. Where is Justin now?"

"He's at his house over on Chestnut Drive."

"What's the number?" Sylvia asked calmly.

"Oh, no, you can't go there, Sylvia." Lines of worry creased Athena's face. "When he left here he was pretty angry. It would be best for me to take you to the airport now."

"No, Athena. I want to talk to Justin. Please give me his address." Sylvia watched as Athena wrote on a slip of paper. She realized Athena was giving her Justin's address against her better judgment, but she took the paper from her. She left the studio and hailed a cab to Justin's home on Chestnut Drive.

Sylvia followed Justin's housekeeper into the library where he was relaxing and reading the evening paper. He glanced up and, for a moment, was at a loss for words. He was shocked to see her standing before him.

"Hello, Justin," she said.

"To what do I owe this honor?" he asked, getting up from the sofa. "I thought you were on your way back to Houston."

"I'd like to talk to you."

"Of course. Please sit down."

"I'd rather stand, but please make yourself comfortable," she said, intending to put him at a disadvantage
by towering over him. He sat back down on the sofa, but
her plan backfired. The defiance she saw in his eyes
told her that he was very much in control.

"You've been very unfair to Athena, Justin," she said,
folding her arms in front of her. She could feel her
courage slowly slipping away, but she was determined
to recite all of the speech she had mentally written
during the cab ride.

"I don't think you're in a position to make that deteri-
nation," he stated impassively. "Whatever happens
between my sister and me is our business."

"On the contrary, Justin. I'm very much involved."

"Only indirectly."

"Justin it doesn't make sense for you not to want
Emary Oaks to handle your work," she argued. "What
are you afraid of?"

Justin got to his feet and slipped his hands into his
pockets. "I have a right to sell or not sell my work to
whomever I please." He walked closer to her and spoke
in a low, angry voice. "And, my dear Lovely Lady, I
guarantee you that I'm not afraid of you or your precious Emary Oaks."

"We could do a lot for you." She took a step
backward.

"Precisely. However, for your information, you can't
do any more for me than I can do for myself." He glared
at her before he turned and walked to the far side of the
room.

"Your arrogance will stand in the way of your success, Justin."

"Then I'll have only myself to blame for my failure,"

he countered. He swiftly covered the space between them and stood directly in front of her. "Do understand this, Sylvia. Don't ever again badger my sister for any more of my work."

"How dare you, Justin." Her voice was husky and angry. Hot tears sprang to her eyes and, although she tried very hard, she could not prevent them from rolling down her cheeks.

"Yes, Sylvia. I'm glad you've finally realized that I do possess the courage to stop you from attempting to run my life."

"You flatter yourself," she said between sobs. "I've never been interested in running your life. I'm only interested in buying your work for Emary Oaks."

"My work is my life," he said.

"All right, Justin," Sylvia said, securing her purse under her arm. "You'll never have to worry about me buying your work again. But I still think you've been unfair to Athena. She loves you very much and, although you don't appreciate her efforts, she's trying hard to help you."

"I don't want the kind of help she's offering." His voice softened as he took her by the shoulders and pulled her to him. "And since you've brought up the subject of love, let's discuss it in more detail. Just what is your relationship with Armand?"

His question angered her even further, and she pulled away from him and walked toward the door. "Armand is not your concern," she said.

"No, he's not, but I'd like to know anyway."

She hesitated at the door and then faced him. "What is your relationship with Polly?" she demanded.

"Leave Polly out of this. We're discussing Armand."

"No, Justin. You're discussing Armand, and I'm leaving."

Justin rushed to her and forcibly pulled her around to face him. "Not yet," he said through tight lips. "You came here to talk, so talk."

"I've said all I have to say."

"Answer my question," Justin demanded, gripping her shoulders tighter.

Sylvia's lips began to tremble and tears streamed down her face. She tried to wriggle out of his grip, but his fingers, like steel claws, held her in place. "There's nothing more to say, Justin."

Reluctantly, he released her shoulders. She walked over to the sofa, sank onto the large, soft cushions and sobbed. Justin walked over and eased down beside her. "I'm sorry, Sylvia," he whispered, slipping his arm around her waist. Exhausted from the past weekend, the drive to Dallas, her long day in the market and their argument, Sylvia rested her head on Justin's shoulder and allowed him to hold her. Tenderly, he caressed her face until her sobbing slowly ceased. After some time, Justin left Sylvia on the sofa. He returned with two glasses of Chablis.

"Truce?" he asked, handing one of the large goblets to her.

"Truce." she whispered.

He sat back down and, like Sylvia, became lost in private thought. In silence, they sipped their wine. Several minutes later, the telephone rang, jarring them back to the present. "It's a long distance call for you, Mr. Udall," Mrs. Bellows announced as she walked into the room.

"I'll take it in my workroom," he told the housekeeper. He turned to Sylvia. "This may take some time, but promise you'll stay and have dinner with me."

"No, Justin. I really should go now." Sylvia put her glass on the side table and got to her feet.

"Please," he persisted. Their eyes locked for a moment. "I want you to stay." He rose from the sofa, walked to the door and paused. "Should I tell Mrs. Bellows to set another place?" he asked.

Slowly, Sylvia nodded her head. "Athena is waiting for me at your studio," she said. "She's supposed to drive me to the airport."

"I'll let Athena know that I'll drive you," he said definitively.

Sylvia nodded again and watched him leave the room. She tucked her legs underneath her and rested her head on the arm rest of the sofa. Before long she had drifted off to sleep.

An hour later, Sylvia woke up stretched out on the sofa. A light blanket was spread over her. She assumed either Justin or Mrs. Bellows had covered her during her sleep. It was late evening and the sun had almost completely slipped behind the trees. She got to her feet and walked to the window. She was looking at the immaculately-landscaped lawn, when she heard someone come into the room.

"Feeling better?" Justin asked, coming to stand beside her.

"Yes, thank you," she answered. I'm embarrassed for falling asleep that way."

"You were very tired, Sylvia," he said. "Come," he reached for her, "dinner is ready."

She followed him out on the terrace where a table was beautifully laid with stuffed deviled crab, a variety of fresh salads and steamed fresh vegetables. Sylvia ate well, surprised she was so hungry.

"The view from here is lovely," she said, gazing out toward an elaborate bird bath. She placed her napkin on the table beside her plate.

"Would you like a tour of the grounds?" Justin asked. We have about an hour of daylight left."

"Oh, I'd love it, Justin."

Hand in hand, they walked out of the intricately-carved back door into the yard. The restored turn-of-the-century mansion sat on an acre and a half of land peppered with huge, stately oak and pine trees. From the back of the house, a winding stone walkway, edged with English ivy and colorful summer flowers, led to a white, delicately-constructed wrought iron gazebo. A small garden occupied a far corner of the yard and displayed an abundance of gold, lavender, pink, white and red blossoms. Evergreen shrubbery accented the complete area.

"The grounds are very beautiful," Sylvia said, as they sat in the gazebo admiring the view. "Do you ever work out here?"

"No," Justin replied, "but I come here often for inspiration."

"A yard as pretty and peaceful as this one should have children playing in it," she said, instantly realizing that she sounded like some silly coquette.

"Agreed," she heard Justin reply, and she could feel his eyes fasten on her.

Sylvia got to her feet hurriedly and started to walk back toward the house. "What's over there?" she asked, pointing to the side of the house.

Around the side of the house was a large, free-form

swimming pool with a natural stone waterfall and coping.

"It's not the creek," Justin smiled, "but you can get a good swim here. Would you like to try it?"

Sylvia laughed softly. "No, I have to get back to Houston. Perhaps some other time."

"I'm going to hold you to that," Justin said, taking her hand once more and leading her back to the house. "But you can't leave before the grand tour of my home."

They entered the east wing of the house through the large French doors of the sunroom. "Justin, this room is just like you," Sylvia said, looking around her.

"Really?"

"Yes. The brick walls and high-arched windows are so ...so ...masterful. Even the giant cactuses are ..." She turned to look at him and cut her sentence short. Justin was smiling at her, amused.

"Did I say something funny?" she asked.

"No," Justin smiled.

She knew her attempt at describing the room had amused him and she became annoyed with herself for her choice of words. They moved on through other beautifully-decorated rooms of the house that had deeply-coffered oak beams, bay windows with low interior shutters, teak floors with butterfly-shaped rosewood keys, and several Spanish fireplaces. Justin's work was displayed throughout the house.

"You have a beautiful home," Sylvia said, after they made their way back to the library.

"I'm sincerely pleased you like it. Our tastes are quite similar, Sylvia."

Their eyes met briefly. "I think I should go now," she said.

"Of course." He drove her to the airport and she boarded a plane for Houston.

Chapter Six

Sylvia, determined not to let the past weekend color her mood, went into work early on Tuesday morning. She zestfully greeted Henrika and the saleswomen, and then settled down to read her mail.

"The Udall canvases are still selling very well," Mary informed her.

The very mention of his name brought to mind a flood of wonderful memories. Sylvia knew she had to forget Justin Udall, but realized it would not be easy.

"Yes, there's growing excitement in the city about his work," Henrika agreed. "Were you able to get him to change his mind about selling to us?"

"I was able to buy ten canvases yesterday," Sylvia said, attempting to sound nonchalant. "However, they are the last we will ever be sold. Sorry, Henrika," she added softly.

"I appreciate your efforts," Henrika said, studying Sylvia closely, "and I'm sorry things didn't work out better with Justin for you or the store."

"Both Emary Oaks and I will manage very well without him," Sylvia replied, attempting a smile but failing.

"I know," Henrika assured her.

Sylvia spent the rest of the week working long hours at the store. Since Henrika insisted that she take Saturday off, she made plans for the day. She refused to allow herself time to think about Justin. She would have lunch and explore the arboretum with Bluma during the day, followed by dinner with Armand that night.

She met Bluma at the mall and they had a light lunch. "It's a relief to see you're no longer driving yourself so hard," Bluma said as they left the restaurant and headed toward the arboretum. "All work and no play," she gave Sylvia a sidelong glance. "I think you know the rest."

"Yes, I know the rest, Bluma," she replied patiently. They drove along the freeway noting the evidence of summer slowly fading into autumn.

"Taking a walk was a great idea," Bluma said, changing the subject. "It's a beautiful day."

Within minutes they were at the arboretum. Sylvia parked the car and they headed for the woods. Choosing one of the many marked trails to follow, they began a leisurely walk through a variety of trees and plants. The trail was bordered with deep ground cover, and the bright afternoon sunlight filtered boldly through full branches of tall trees, casting dancing shadows all about them.

"Justin has huge oak and pine trees just like these in his yard," Sylvia said, breaking the silence.

"I know."

"You can see his bird bath from the terrace and all kinds of birds gather there."

"It sounds like a delightful place."

"It is. He landscaped the grounds himself, and even chose the flowers for the garden." They stopped for a moment and read a marker that identified a small bush as a `black haw shrub'. "Did I tell you about Justin's house in Dallas?"

"Every detail," Bluma answered. They looked at each other and giggled.

"Justin really is a rather nice person," Sylvia continued, shoving her hands into her pockets.

"From what you've told me about him I think I'd have to agree with you." Bluma picked up some dried oak, pecan and redbud leaves and crushed them. As they both watched, she allowed the wind to take the small pieces from her fingers. "I'd like to meet him."

"You'd like his sensitivity and wit, Bluma."

They crossed a narrow wooden bridge over a small stream of water, and took a new path that lead deeper into the woods.

"Do you remember the words of the songs he wrote for you?" Bluma asked.

Sylvia looked embarrassed. "Yes. I wrote them down," she admitted.

"I'll bet you even learned to strum the tunes on your guitar." Bluma gave her a mischievous smile.

"No comment," Sylvia laughed.

"You've got it bad, girl."

"I'll recover."

"Why don't you call him?"

"Never. Polly may answer the phone."

"You still haven't found out about their relationship?" Bluma asked, surprised.

"No, every time I ask him about Polly, he asks me about Armand."

"And what do you tell him?"

"Nothing."

"Sounds like you're both being a little stubborn."

"I know," Sylvia sighed, "but I wish I could get him to tell me how he feels about her."

"Just as he'd like to know how you feel about Armand."

"Yes."

"Why don't you ask Athena about them. She seems to like you an awful lot."

"That would be tacky, Bluma."

"I don't think so."

"Forget it."

After their walk, Sylvia went home to dress for her dinner date with Armand, hoping she had not made a mistake by accepting his invitation.

"I was afraid you would turn me down when I called on Thursday," Armand said nervously. His sad brown eyes surveyed Sylvia carefully. "You've made me very happy by having dinner with me tonight." They sat having after-dinner coffee in a large, crowded restaurant where an elderly gentleman played show tunes on a grand piano.

"I've always enjoyed being with you, Armand," Sylvia replied, "and I hope we can always be friends." She felt relaxed and comfortable in the restaurant, and was pleased Armand had chosen it for dinner.

"How are your parents?" he asked casually.

"They're doing very well," Sylvia answered. "I spoke with them by phone last night."

"Have you told them yet that our marriage has been postponed?"

Sylvia's eyes flew open in amazement, and for a moment she had trouble forming her words. "What do you mean postponed, Armand?" I thought you understood that I will never marry you."

"You did say that, Sylvia," he said, stirring his coffee absently, "but I think you're just a little confused right now. In a few weeks you'll be over your infatuation with Justin and ready to go on with our wedding plans."

Sylvia fought the anger and guilt that Armand had evoked in her. "I'm quite capable of knowing my own mind, Armand," she said, struggling to control the emotion in her voice. "I've given our relationship plenty of thought and I know without a shadow of a doubt we can never be married. I don't love you." She quickly placed the back of her hand over her lips and closed her eyes, dreading to see the pain on Armand's face. To her surprise, however, her words seemed to have had a contrary effect on him.

"We'll see," he said. Although her searching eyes could still discern sadness in his face, Armand seemed to have gained new hope and strength. His optimistic attitude made Sylvia uneasy.

* * *

November arrived slowly and without fanfare. Sylvia had fallen into a routine of working long hours at the store, jogging, and occasionally having lunch or dinner with Bluma or Henrika. From time to time, Armand called. Although Sylvia talked with him by phone, she refused his invitations to dinner or the theater. She was determined not to encourage him in any way.

Thanksgiving Day was approaching and Sylvia had

not made plans for the holiday. She had removed the
small card from the envelope she received in the mail
and read it several times. She knew what she would do.
However, she had told herself, she would mull over the
issue for several days before acting on her decision. She
had finally walked purposefully to the mailbox and
dropped the note through the slot, accepting Copland
and Athena's invitation to spend the Thanksgiving
weekend with them in their Dallas home.

Sylvia arrived in Dallas on Wednesday evening and
found the DeForest home festive and gay. To her
delight, they had been invited out to dinner and the
theater by Paul Wright and his friend, Gretta, which
gave her holiday weekend the perfect beginning. For
the first time in weeks, she found herself laughing
easily, and thoroughly enjoying the company of others.
She realized she had made the right decision by accepting the DeForest's invitation for the weekend. She felt
completely happy and relaxed.

Thanksgiving Day dinner was scheduled for early
evening. Sylvia and her hosts spent the morning and
afternoon chatting and reading the newspaper. Then
they dressed to meet the other guests. Sylvia pulled a
white, long-sleeved lace blouse over her head and
adjusted the deep V-cut neckline. She stepped into a
pair of pearl gray, silk crepe evening slacks and matching gray silk pumps. She combed her hair, allowing
full, loose curls to fall carelessly about her shoulders.
After dabbing perfume behind her ears and on her
wrists, she went out to find her hosts.

Copland, dressed in a dark suit and crisp white shirt,
was in the living room selecting music for the evening.
Athena was in the dining room putting the finishing

touches on the centerpiece. She was elegant in an aquamarine, long silk dress with tiny buttons and long sleeves.

Sylvia helped Athena with the centerpiece. Afterwards they went to the kitchen to see about dinner. Mrs. Grady, the housekeeper, assured them that everything was progressing according to schedule. Back in the living room, they waited for their guests. The first to arrive were Mike and Sandy Wilder, followed by Paul Wright and Gretta. Several other couples came in. They were all enjoying the evening, when the last couple arrived—Justin, with Polly holding tightly to his arm. When Sylvia saw them walk across the room together, a sharp pain pieced her heart. She quickly turned her head and, momentarily, her eyes met Paul's. At that moment, she realized her love for Justin was no longer a secret.

After a short period, Mrs. Grady announced dinner, and the small, elegant group went into the dining room to share the traditional Thanksgiving dinner. With the exception of a few barbs by Polly intended for Sylvia, the mood around the table was light and cheerful. Sylvia wondered why Polly felt the need to hurt her, since she had obviously won Justin's heart.

After dinner—which was superb—the party moved back to the living room where they listened to soft music and chatted congenially. In spite of her aching heart, Sylvia was able to join in the lively chatter. It was obvious the DeForest's guests found her charming. She was relieved her happy facade was convincing—to everyone, that is, except Paul.

All evening Justin seemed unaware of Sylvia's presence. When he had to address her directly, he did so as if he were speaking to a stranger. Once during the evening Sylvia permitted her gaze to hold Justin's. The look in his eyes was the same sadness she had observed in Armand's on recent occasions. She wondered why he was unhappy.

The evening drew toward an end, and Justin and Polly were the first to leave. Slowly, everyone else followed their lead. As Copland, Athena and Sylvia stood at the door saying their goodbyes to their last guests, Paul and Gretta, Justin came up the walk alone. He mumbled a few words to Paul and Gretta, and addressed his sister.

"I think I left my wallet here," he said. "I'd like to look for it."

Athena, who was standing in the doorway, stepped aside, allowing him to enter the house. "By all means look for your wallet, Justin," she said. She exchanged glances with Copland and they closed the door and discreetly left the room. Sylvia attempted to follow them, but Justin stopped her.

"Please stay, Sylvia, I'd like to talk to you." His deep voice was thick with emotion.

Sylvia, standing in the middle of the living room floor, slid her hands into her pants pockets. "Where's Polly?" she asked, acrimoniously. "Isn't she in a talkative mood?"

"I took Polly home." Justin moved across the floor so quickly, he frightened her. "I want to talk to you," he said, his face tormented. He took her by the shoulders and drew her to him.

"You said talk, Justin." Impassioned by his touch, she tried to wriggle out of his grip.

Justin dropped his hands from her shoulders and walked away. "Where is Armand this weekend?" he demanded acidly.

"Don't concern yourself with Armand, Justin," Sylvia answered with an equal degree of sharpness in her voice. "But if you must know, he is in Louisiana on business."

"Why didn't you go to him for the holiday?" His dark expressive eyes searched her face.

"Aren't we nosey," Sylvia hissed. Not knowing how to answer Justin, she walked over to a side table and ran her fingers across its top. "I have no desire to disturb Armand while he's working," she finally said, and then realized how cold she sounded.

"You certainly sound like a woman in love," Justin spat the words at her.

"Look Justin," Sylvia began slowly. "I have no desire to discuss my personal life with you. If you'd like to talk to me about selling some of your works to Emary Oaks, I'm all ears. Otherwise, we have nothing to say to each other."

"On the contrary, Lovely Lady," Justin said, moving slowly toward her. "We have plenty to say to each other."

Sylvia took a step backward and found herself pinned against the wall. Justin moved closer. He stood looking down at her for a few moments, then slipped his arms around her waist and pulled her tight against him. Instantly his lips found hers. Sylvia's lips parted and Justin's demanding kisses seemed to delve into her very soul. Her arms encircled his neck and her brightly-tipped fingers dug deeply into the thickness of his curly hair. Justin's nimble-fingered hands began a slow, masterful massage of her back and neck. His breathing grew heavy, as one hand moved inside the front of her blouse and lovingly stroked her breasts. Sylvia totally surrendered to his demands.

"Is this what you're looking for, Justin?" Athena called from the hallway. Justin released Sylvia just as Athena entered the room clutching a wallet between her fingers. Without looking back or uttering another word, he took the wallet from his sister and walked out of the house.

Sylvia's encounter with Justin on Thanksgiving Day had thrown her back into a blue mood. Although she tried hard to recapture her lighthearted disposition, the next two days with Athena and Copland were difficult. Athena was aware of her unhappy state, and attempted to cheer her up. They spent the remainder of the weekend exploring Dallas.

Sylvia elected to revisit two of her favorite places, though she had been there many times before. First, they went to the John Fitzgerald Kennedy Memorial. The white concrete cenotaph was erected by the people of Dallas as a tribute to the President who was assassinated close by in 1963. The monument was designed with walls to shut out the outside world, and was open at the top to allow communion only with God. They remained there for more than an hour. After lunch, they went to the Dallas Museum of Fine Arts.

On Saturday, Copland was in a giddy mood and suggested they go to Six Flags Over Texas. Athena and Sylvia liked the idea. Within minutes they were in jeans and sweaters and headed for the amusement park.

The 150-acre landscaped entertainment center depicted Texas under the flags of France, Spain, Mexico, the Republic of Texas, the Confederate States of America and the United States. Each section had food and entertainment in keeping with its era. In the park were more than 100 rides and attractions, which included a 200-foot parachute drop, double-loop roller coaster, log flume ride and a runaway mine train. They spent the entire day in the park and had a wonderful time.

The next morning, Athena went to Sylvia's room, carrying a pot of coffee. "We're so pleased you spent this weekend with us, Sylvia," she said, filling a cup and handing it to her. "We've enjoyed having you here so very much."

"You and Copland have been terrific, Athena," Sylvia replied. "Thank you for inviting me."

Sylvia sipped slowly from the hot cup of coffee and watched as Athena nervously paced the floor. "I know how you feel about Justin, Sylvia," she said softly, "and I know he feels the same way about you."

Sylvia, startled by Athena's remark, wanted to deny her feelings for Justin, but she knew she would only sound foolish. She set her cup on the nightstand, and began taking her things from drawers and the closet and placing them in her bag. Feeling a little embarrassed that her feelings for Justin were so obvious, Sylvia did not take her eyes from her packing as she spoke to Athena. Had she walked around all weekend looking like a love-sick schoolgirl over Justin? The thought that she probably had, spurred her into throwing her belongings into her bag even faster. If Athena could see her love for Justin, then so could he. Perhaps that's why he felt arrogant enough to toy with her affections. The idea was almost too much for her to bear.

"I think you're mistaken about Justin," she said. "He's not interested in me. He's involved with Polly."

"I'm neither wrong about you nor Justin," Athena said emphatically. "And don't worry about Polly."

Sylvia stopped and looked at Athena. "But she's always with Justin and one would assume ..."

"Stop assuming, Sylvia. Justin is not romantically interested in Polly."

"Has he told you that?" Sylvia could feel her stomach muscles tighten as she waited for the answer.

Athena caught her hand and they both sat on the corner of the bed. "Polly is a dear friend of our family, and has been going through a trying experience for the past few months. Her twin brother, who was an artist and very close to Justin, recently died from a terminal illness. Polly hasn't recovered from the shock of his death, and being close to Justin seems to ease the pain for her. Because Justin and her brother were such close friends, he feels he should see her through this difficult period. Be patient, Sylvia. Things will work out. You'll see."

Sylvia wanted to believe Athena, but for some reason she could not. She wondered if Justin and Polly's relationship had begun as Athena had described it and later developed into something more. Probably so, and they just hadn't told Athena. "Thanks for caring," she said, kissing her friend on the cheek.

After breakfast, she returned to Houston.

Chapter Seven

December had always been a busy and exciting
month at the store, and this year was no exception.
Basic merchandise bought for the Nook of International
Treasures was moving fast. The last shipment of
Justin's work had sold soon after it was placed on the
floor. No day passed without customers requesting
canvases by the artist. It was becoming increasingly
difficult to convince them the store no longer carried his
work. Other native Texas arts and crafts were selling
well also, and Sylvia was gratified her new venture had
been an overwhelming success.

However, victory did not prevail in her private life.
Her heart still ached for Justin. Nevertheless, she made
plans to meet new people. She joined a vintage car club
and resumed French lessons at the nearby university. A
couple of times a week, she played racquetball at the
club and occasionally accepted dinner invitations from
admirers.

Now on this crisp December day, she found herself
driving down Montrose Boulevard to meet Armand.
After his return from Louisiana, he had resumed his
periodic calls. It was during his last call that she had

agreed to meet him at the Fine Arts Museum to see a special exhibit from France.

She parked her car and crossed the street. Armand was waiting for her just inside the door. She rushed into the museum accompanied by a cold gust of wind. "Hi," she said.

"Hi," he answered, smiling happily. "It's good to see you again, Sylvia."

"Thanks. It's good seeing you, Armand."

He helped her off with her coat, and they moved through the crowd to the stairs. Armand looked well and happy, and she could tell by his confident manner that he had some good news he wanted to share with her. Feeling sure marriage to her was now out of his mind and they were currently just friends again, Sylvia walked leisurely with Armand through the spacious exhibition rooms.

"I love the French impressionists," she said, gazing at a large canvas of a family in a Parisian park scene.

"Yes, I do, too. Their work makes me feel so light."

They strolled through the rooms for two hours and then left the exhibit. "How about a cup of hot chocolate?" Armand asked, guiding Sylvia toward the coffee shop.

"You know my weakness," she smiled.

As they drank their chocolate, Sylvia wondered how long it would take Armand to tell her his good news. He was still wearing a happy, confident expression, but he was taking his time about revealing his secret.

"Would you like more?" Armand asked, when she had finished her chocolate.

"No. I've had enough." They left the museum and crossed the street to the parking lot. "Thanks for inviting me to the exhibit," Sylvia said. "I've enjoyed the afternoon."

"Let's not end our day yet," Armand replied. "Let's take a walk down to Bell Park."

"All right." Bell Park was a lovely little pocket park several blocks from the museum, and Sylvia assumed Armand would give her his good news there.

As they walked along, Armand took Sylvia's hand in his. The implication made her uncomfortable. She began a mental debate with herself over how to best handle the situation without causing hard feelings. At that time, Armand looked up at her and smiled.

"When will we set the date?" he asked with sincerity.

His words momentarily paralyzed her. "What do you mean?" she demanded.

Armand lifted happy, sparkling eyes to Sylvia. "I can tell you've come to your senses concerning Justin, Sylvia. Now we can go on with our wedding plans." His smile was warm and sweet.

Realizing she would have to dissolve a friendship that had existed since childhood, Sylvia's eyes focused on a distant building. She had been foolish to believe they could remain friends after their broken engagement. How wrong she had been to think Armand had made new plans for his life that didn't include her. Hadn't she made it clear she couldn't marry him? Was he looking so well and happy because he had decided they could now go on with plans for a wedding? Armand was assuming again, and this time she couldn't allow him to go on with his fantasy.

"I haven't changed my mind, Armand," she said evenly. Her heart thumped in her chest. She was both angry and sad that she had to go through the ordeal of rejecting Armand again. "I don't love you and we can never be married."

"Is it Justin?"

"Justin has nothing to do with my feelings for you."

"Do you love him?" Armand demanded.

Their eyes met for a moment. "Yes," she whispered.

"I see." His voice was filled with anger and disappointment. "Then there's nothing more to say, Sylvia." He turned on his heel and walked away.

Sylvia continued her walk to the park. She found a bench facing a small stream with a wooden bridge across it and sat down. Without warning, she began to cry. Violent sobs shook her body as tears streamed down her face. She cried for the loss of her friendship with Armand, and she cried for herself.

* * *

"I'm in desperate need of a favor," Henrika said to Sylvia, who had just returned from lunch.

Sylvia slipped her handbag into the bottom drawer of her desk. "What's the problem?" she asked.

"Heller's Antique Shop in Dallas has refused to send me a vase I need for one of my mother-in-law's Christmas gifts. They're no longer taking holiday telephone orders because they can't guarantee prompt delivery. Sylvia, please pick it up for me in the morning. I can't leave the store tomorrow because of my lunch date with Bill Richards."

"Who's Bill Richards?"

"Oh, remember I told you about him. He's going to remodel the Nook of International Treasures at the beginning of next year. He insists that I see him tomorrow to look at the plans."

"Oh, Henrika," Sylvia said, staring in the mirror of her makeup compact as she patted her hair in place, "I'm not in the mood to go to Dallas tomorrow. And besides, they're expecting bad weather there on the weekend."

"I know," Henrika said hastily, "but they don't expect the weather to change until Saturday night. Tomorrow is Friday. You'll be back by then."

"I don't know, Henrika."

"Please, Sylvia. You're the only person I can ask."

The next morning, Sylvia boarded a plane in Houston amid dancing snow flurries, and deplaned in Dallas under a steady snowfall. Streets were icy and congested, but she managed to get to the antique shop and purchase the vase for Henrika. Having a few hours to while away before her flight back to Houston, she decided to go shopping at Neiman-Marcus. The store was packed and it was difficult for her to move about easily, but she was able to find several items she wanted. By the time she left the store, the snow had become heavier and had shrouded the city in a white blanket.

The streets were bustling with Christmas shoppers. Sylvia joined them as they darted in and out of stores, and strolled along the sidewalks looking in the gaily-decorated shop windows. Unintentionally, she soon found herself standing in front of the Udall Gallery.

Athena, who had been watching the snow from a window, spotted her and ran to the shop door. "Sylvia," she called. "What are you doing standing out there in this weather? Come inside," she said, holding the door open for her. Sylvia went into the studio and the two women embraced. "It's wonderful to see you," she continued. "Why didn't you call?"

"I've only been here a few hours," Sylvia answered, "and as soon as I can get a cab, I'm going back to the airport. This is just a one-day trip."

"But haven't you heard," Athena asked worriedly, "planes have been grounded and roads are being closed. We're expecting pretty rough weather for the next twenty-four hours. Copland is on his way to pick me up, now. We're going to try to make it to the ranch before it gets too bad. Come with us, Sylvia."

"I can't do that," Sylvia said. "Are you sure they've grounded planes, Athena."

"I'm positive."

"But the snowstorm wasn't expected until tomorrow night," Sylvia insisted.

"They miscalculated," Athena informed her.

At that moment, Copland pulled in front of the studio and Athena began securing the doors and windows. "You might as well come with us," she said. "You wouldn't want to be snowbound in a hotel full of strangers."

Sylvia reluctantly consented to go along with Copland and Athena. She climbed into the back seat of their car with her boxes and bags. The drive to the ranch was rough. The snowfall became progressively heavier as they drove farther north out of the city. Visibility was difficult and there were several accidents along the road.

"Why are you going to the ranch in this weather?" Sylvia asked. "Wouldn't it have been easier and safer to go to your house in Dallas?"

Copland laughed. "Yes, Sylvia, it would have been

both sensible and easier to stay in Dallas, but I'm kind of unreasonable when it comes to my horses. I rest easier if I take care of them myself when the weather is severe."

"And its always so beautiful at the ranch when it snows," Athena added. "I'm sure you'll love being there, Sylvia."

They arrived at the ranch exactly three hours after they had left Dallas. The one and a half-hour drive had taken twice as long in the snow.

When they walked into the living room, they were surprised to see Polly curled up in a chair, gazing out of the window. "Isn't it beautiful?" she cooed. She eyed Sylvia with chilliness. "What are you doing here?" she asked.

Sylvia looked at Polly and began to remember the conversation with Athena at Thanksgiving. Still, questions rambled through her mind about Polly's relationship with Justin. Did Polly need Justin to ease the pain of her brother's death? Or was that just an excuse to get closer to him? Was Justin just successfully hiding his love for Polly from Athena and Copland? But why would he? What difference does it make? Obviously, he is not interested in me, Sylvia thought, sighing deeply.

"Hi." Justin walked into the room carrying an armful of logs to build a fire. "I'm glad to see you again, Sylvia," he said, giving her an admiring glance. Before she could open her mouth to answer him, he turned to his sister and brother-in-law. "I tried to reach you two several times today, but the lines were out. I wanted to let you know I had come to the ranch in case you didn't want to risk driving out in the storm."

"Thanks, man, but you know I would've worried myself sick over the horses if I hadn't come to the ranch tonight," Copland replied.

"Yes, I know," Justin said. "But I thought I'd let you know, anyway." He got the fire going and stood in front of it warming his hands. "Are the roads very bad?" he asked.

"They're getting dangerous," Athena answered. "You're not thinking of going back to Dallas tonight, are you?"

"No, but Polly needs to get back," he said thoughtfully.

"You can't drive back in this weather, Polly," Athena advised her. "Please consider staying the night."

"Oh, thank you, Athena," Polly sang cheerfully.

Copland slipped out of his parka and threw it on a chair. "Is everything all right with you, Polly?" he asked. "You drove out in such severe weather."

"It wasn't that bad this afternoon," Polly answered sweetly. "And since the storm wasn't expected until tomorrow night, I thought it would be safe to drive out for a couple of hours."

"We didn't hear the revised weather forecast until about twenty minutes ago," Justin added. "We had no idea the roads would be too dangerous to travel this quickly."

Polly eased to the edge of her chair and attempted to gain favor with Copland and Athena. "I hadn't seen Justin for two weeks," she said, and shot a nervous glance in Sylvia's direction. "I just wanted to come out to see if he needed anything."

Sylvia had not opened her mouth since walking into the room. She sat on the sofa directly in front of the fireplace and listened to the verbal exchange with interest. She had fixed her eyes on her fingers, which were laced together and resting in her lap, and she could feel Justin's eyes fixed on her. As she sat there enjoying the warmth of the fire, she decided not to allow Polly nor Justin to ruin her stay at the ranch. Since she was there, she would be as pleasant as possible to both of them, and as soon as the weather permitted, she would leave. With that resolution firm in her mind, she lifted her lashes and smiled.

"Now that everyone is warm and settled," Athena said, "perhaps we should give some thought to dinner. What should we have?"

"What do we have?" Copland asked.

"I think we're pretty well-stocked."

"Then, what do you feel like eating?" he continued. "I don't have an appetite for anything special."

"Neither do I," Athena answered. She stretched lazily in front of the cozy fire.

"I think Sylvia should plan and prepare dinner for us. I'll bet she's a good little cook," Polly said sarcastically.

An amused expression eased across Sylvia's face as she turned slowly to gaze at Polly. "I'm an excellent cook," she said, getting up from the sofa. "I'd be delighted to plan and prepare dinner." She walked toward the kitchen with four pairs of surprised eyes following her.

"I wouldn't dream of allowing you to cook dinner," Athena said, getting to her feet.

"I'll cook," Justin said, rushing behind his sister.

"This is all kind of silly," Copland mused, watching the room empty, "but I guess I might as well join the group."

In the kitchen, Sylvia opened the refrigerator and cupboards as if she were in her own home. She took boned chicken breasts from the refrigerator, sprinkled them with seasoned salt and white pepper, placed them in a skillet of hot olive oil, added freshly-chopped garlic, freshly-squeezed lemon juice, covered the skillet and allowed the meat to cook slowly. She began boiling a pot of rice.

"That looks delicious," Athena observed. "What vegetable would be good with it?"

"Why don't you grill these, Athena," Sylvia replied, handing her fresh ripe tomatoes. She looked up and found Copland and Justin gazing at her blankly. "Justin, you can make a salad," she said, and he walked over to the refrigerator.

"Spinach or watercress?" he asked, holding the door open.

"Spinach with boiled eggs, mushrooms and onion rings."

"Right."

She looked at Copland and smiled. "I guess dessert is left up to you." She looked around the kitchen and spotted a bowl of bananas on the counter. "What can you do with those in a hurry?" she asked, pointing to the fruit.

"Flame them," Copland answered with a wink.

"Terrific."

Polly sat in the living room alone. Her cute remark, intended to embarrass Sylvia, had backfired. Reluctantly, she went to the kitchen to join them.

"Decided to help?" Copland asked when he saw her.

"Yes," she smiled. "I'm afraid Sylvia may turn out to be like the Little Red Hen. If you don't work, you don't eat. What can I do?"

"Ask Sylvia," Justin said, busily washing the spinach. "She's the one giving out assignments."

"What would you like me to do, Sylvia?" Polly asked begrudgingly.

Sylvia stifled a smile. "Polly, you're such a dear," she said, "and I just adore your little analogies." She turned to Polly and wrinkled her nose. "Why don't you try setting the table and filling the water glasses with water."

Polly glared at her before opening the cabinet for dishes.

"We'll eat in the breakfast nook," Athena said, indicating the glassed-in room just off the kitchen. "That way we can watch the snow." She showed Polly which table linen and dishes to use, and turned back to her work.

Everyone except Polly seemed to be in high spirits. They laughed and joked as each one prepared his dish. In no time, dinner was on the table. The jovial mood continued as they ate the delicious meal, each one complimenting the other on how well each dish had turned out. Polly pouted throughout dinner.

After dinner, Polly announced she would do the dishes.

"Thanks, Polly, I'll help you," Athena offered.

"I enjoy cooking, but I hate cleaning the kitchen afterwards," Justin said.

"Me, too," Copland agreed.

Sylvia could see Polly's disappointment as Justin and Copland left the kitchen. "I'll help too," she said, feeling a little sorry for Polly.

Before long they had finished the dishes and joined

the two men, who were lounging about in the living room. They sat around the fire chatting for about an hour before Athena decided it was time to start making sleeping arrangements for Polly and Sylvia.

"Polly, since you and Sylvia will share the guest quarters, I'd like to make sure you'll have everything you'll need for the night," Athena said, getting to her feet. "Why don't you both come with me now?"

Sylvia rose from her chair, walked over to where Athena was standing, and waited for Polly to follow. However, Polly remained seated.

"Do you mean I have to share the guest quarters with Sylvia?" she asked. Obvious disgust showed on her face.

This time Polly's rudeness surprised Athena. For a moment she just stared at the young woman. "Yes, Polly," she answered, "the guest quarters is large enough for both of you."

Pouting, Polly rose, took her sweater from a chair and slowly walked toward them.

"Athena," Justin said, attempting to appease Polly, "Sylvia can take my room for the night. I'll sleep in my studio. Go with Athena now, Polly, so that she can help you with whatever you may need," he said. "I'll show Sylvia to my room. You can come by when you finish with Polly," he told his sister.

Polly shrugged and followed Athena, while Justin led Sylvia to his wing of the ranch house. It was larger than her condominium, and beautifully decorated in tones of cream, beige and green. The furniture was massive pieces of dark wood and several of Justin's canvases hung on the walls.

"I hadn't realized the house was this big," Sylvia said

when she walked into the living area. "How many rooms do you have here?"

Justin took her by the hand and began showing her through his wing of the house. "I have a living and dining area, a library, a bedroom and bathroom and a full kitchen."

"It's beautiful," Sylvia said, gazing out the window that extended the length of the living room. "Who designed it?"

"Athena and I decided we wanted the house built this way," he said. "We felt that, aesthetically, one large house on the land would be more attractive than two smaller ones. So we agreed to build two separate houses around a common living area. That way, we can maintain our privacy, yet share the ranch comfortably."

"With all of this space, Justin, why are you going to your studio to sleep. I wouldn't mind sleeping on the sofa."

"There's an apartment above my studio," he said. "The bed there is very comfortable." He walked over to some beautiful, highly-polished wood cabinets. "Would you like a brandy?" he asked.

"Sounds good," Sylvia said, as she sat down on a deep green posh sofa.

She watched Justin pour the brandies. As he passed by the stereo equipment on his way back with the drinks, he pressed a button and the sweet sounds of Wes Montgomery floated into the room. Justin sat down beside her. For a while they only listened to the music and sipped their drinks.

"Why did you come to Dallas this weekend?" he asked, breaking the silence. "Isn't the buying season over for the store?"

"I'm afraid I'm an errand girl today instead of a working woman," Sylvia confessed. "I came to Dallas to pick up a package for Henrika. I had planned to return to Houston about four o'clock this afternoon."

"And now you're snowbound with me," Justin teased mischievously.

"Yes, I'm snowbound with you, Polly, Copland and Athena. It's all so romantic." She returned his mischievous glance.

"Some things have a way of not working out, don't they," he said, getting up and walking to the window. He stood for a while gazing out before beckoning for her to join him. She rose from her seat and went to his side. "Look," he said, pointing toward some trees in the distance. Sylvia could see several small animals with bushy tails, who were about the size of a medium-sized dog. "Foxes," Justin told her.

"Will they bother the horses?" she asked.

"No. The horses are safe. Copland has seen to that." He turned around to face her and their eyes locked. "I'm very glad you're here, Sylvia," he said huskily. He pulled her into his arms and kissed her tenderly. "I'm so very, very glad," he whispered against her throat.

A soft rapping at the door interrupted them. "It's me," Athena said, opening the door. "I've brought your things, Sylvia." She walked down the hall to the bedroom and placed the young woman's bags and boxes on the bed. Sylvia reluctantly removed herself from Justin's arms and followed Athena. "Here are some things I thought you might need," she said. "Would you like me to get anything else for you?"

Sylvia looked at the articles that had been placed on

the bed and nightstand. "I think you've covered everything," she said. "Thank you Athena."

"You're welcome," Athena said, leaving the room. "We'll see you in the morning. "Goodnight, Justin," she called, and closed the door quietly behind her.

"I need to get a couple of things before I leave," Justin said, coming into the bedroom. He took some articles out of a bureau drawer and tucked them under his arm. He opened another drawer and took out a pair of white silk pajamas and threw them on the bed. "If Athena forgot to bring you something to sleep in," he said, "these should keep you warm tonight. Sleep well, Lovely Lady." He kissed her lightly on the lips.

Sylvia followed him to the living room. When he had gone, she turned off the music and the lights. She wandered back to the window, gazed out and saw Justin as he walked the path to his studio and disappeared inside. Her eyes traveled out to where they had spotted the foxes and the area was deserted. For a long time, she watched the snow fall gently to the ground. Her mind grasped and lingered on thoughts of Justin. Again their paths had crossed, and again they had been inadvertently drawn to each other. Oh, how very deeply she loved him.

Tired, Sylvia went in to dress for bed. Although Athena was thoughtful enough to bring her a nightshirt to sleep in, she chose to slip into the white silk pajamas Justin had thrown on the bed. She realized she was being infantile and romantic, but somehow wearing his clothes made her feel close to him. She crawled between the beige, white and green plaid sheets of his antique, four-poster bed and pulled the covers up tight around her. Staring at the ceiling, she wondered if

Justin had ever shared this bed with Polly. The idea made the muscles in her stomach tighten, and she rolled onto her side and tried to push the thought from her mind. She adjusted the covers and caught a whiff of Justin's crisp, piney aftershave lotion, and a tiny shiver ran down her spine. Allowing her fingers to creep to the tiny, navy blue monogram on the pocket of the pajama top, she wondered what life would be like for Mrs. Justin Udall. A smile pulled at her lips and she curled up into a warm, comfortable ball. Evemtually, she fell asleep.

The next morning, Sylvia dressed in the red sweater and slacks she had bought on sale at Neiman-Marcus the day before. She went quietly to the kitchen, made breakfast for herself and enjoyed it in the breakfast room, where she gazed out at the freshly-fallen snow. After she had finished, she cleared away the dishes and went to the living room.

"Good morning, sleepy head," Justin said. "You were about to get left behind."

"Left?" Sylvia was surprised. "I thought I was the only one up."

"You're the last one up," Justin laughed. "We're about to take a walk. Would you like to join us?"

"No thanks. I think I'll call the airport and see if I can get a flight out this afternoon."

"You can't get a flight out yet," Justin informed her, stuffing his gloves into his jacket pocket, "and you can't get to Dallas. The roads have been closed by the highway patrol. You're stuck here with us today,

Sylvia," he smiled.

"The storm is over, isn't it?" she asked anxiously.

"Yes, it wasn't as severe or as prolonged as they predicted. Get your coat," he said. "You'll enjoy the walk."

"Well, well, well. If it isn't Little Red Riding Hood, or should I call you Sleeping Beauty," Polly crooned, buttoning up her coat as she came into the living room. She walked over to Justin and attached herself to his arm.

"I think both would fit, Clever Polly," Sylvia said, going to get her coat. "Don't wait for me, Justin," she called over her shoulder. "I'll catch up with you as soon as I'm dressed."

She went back to the bedroom and sank into an overstuffed chair by the window. The thought of spending another day with Polly made her weary. However, she had no choice. With great effort, she pulled on her snow boots, put on her fur jacket and left the house. Not wanting to find Polly and Justin, she walked to the stables to see the horses. Copland and his ranch hand, Pete, were busy grooming the beautiful, sleek animals.

"I think that's the one I rode the last time I was here," she said, indicating the horse Pete was brushing.

"Hi," Copland said.

"Yes, this is the horse, Miss Sylvia," Pete informed her. "This is Sassy Lady."

"She's beautiful," Sylvia commented. "Do you need any help?"

"Yes, you can groom Chancellor," Copland said, handing her a currycomb. "Have you ever groomed a horse before?" he asked.

"When I was a little girl my uncle used to let me help him with his horses," she answered. "I think I remember the basic procedure, but I was never any good at cleaning the hooves."

"That's okay, Pete will take care of his feet."

Sylvia took the rubber comb and began rubbing Chancellor's head. She worked her way back on his near side, including his legs, with circular motions. She then went to the off side and repeated the same procedure.

"Hey, you're pretty good at this," Copland teased her. "If you ever want a job as a ranch hand, let me know."

"I sure will," she said. She took a coarse brush and began brushing off the loose dirt and dust.

"So here's where you've been hiding," Athena said, walking up beside her. "We've been looking for you."

"Good morning, Athena," Sylvia said. "I'm having a grand time grooming Chancellor."

"He looks terrific," Athena replied, "but you can clean the horses any time. Both of you come and enjoy the snow."

Copland and Sylvia left the grooming for Pete to finish and followed Athena.

"What did you have in mind?" he asked, draping his arm around his wife's shoulders. "I'll bet you want to build a snowman," he laughed.

"That would be fun," Athena said. "Let's find Justin and Polly. They may want to help."

When they walked out into the brilliant sunlight, they saw Justin and Polly strolling along out toward the grassland a short distance ahead of them. As they began discussing where they would build the snowman, Sylvia bent over, scooped up two handfuls of snow and formed a snowball. Athena and Copland automatically stopped and watched her, questioningly. Sylvia aimed and hurled her missile, hitting her target, Justin, squarely between the shoulder blades. Justin wheeled around and stared blankly at the threesome behind him. The young woman then hurriedly made another snowball. This time she struck him in the chest. Justin, refusing to let Sylvia get away with her mischief, reached down for some snow just as she managed to get another snowball off, which promptly collided with his head. Justin dismissed the idea of making a snowball. With the swift grace of a tiger, he advanced toward his assailant. Laughing hysterically, Sylvia took off in a trot toward the open fields. She ran like a graceful gazelle through the snow, with Justin close on her heels. Crawling through the fence, she made her way across the grassland, but found the snow too deep and restricting. Justin caught her coattail once, but was unable to hold on, and she made her way back to the fence. Intending to climb over it, she stepped into a deep hole covered with ice and fell.

"My ankle," she screamed, grabbing her left leg. "My ankle."

Justin was at her side within seconds. He clutched her to him and attempted to massage her ankle through her boot.

"Get her inside," Athena yelled to him. "Hurry." Justin picked Sylvia up in his arms and she clung to him like a hurt, frightened child.

"Can you manage?" Copland asked.

"Yes," Justin answered, carrying her easily. "I'm sorry, Sylvia," he whispered against her cheek. "I'm sorry." He carried her into the house and gently placed her on the sofa.

Athena rushed over to her and began examining her ankle. "It doesn't seem to be broken," Athena said, "but we'd better let Dr. Patterson take a few X-rays to be sure. I'll go and call him."

"But how will I get to a doctor?" Sylvia asked, grimacing from the pain shooting up her leg. "The roads are all impassable."

"Don't worry, Sylvia," Justin said, brushing the snow from her hair. "The doctor is only five miles from here and we can get you there in the four-wheel drive."

"Everything's set," Athena said coming back into the room. "The doctor will be waiting for us. I'm going with you," she said, pulling on her coat again.

"Hang tough, Sylvia," Copland said with a smile, "you'll be okay."

"I know," she said, gripping Justin's hand tighter in an attempt to ease the pain.

Polly, who had been watching the events very closely, walked over to Sylvia. "I hope your ankle is not too seriously hurt," she said drily.

"Thanks, Polly."

Justin left to get the jeep and brought it to the front of the house. He then gathered Sylvia into his arms and took her to the car. After he had made sure Sylvia was comfortable, Athena crawled into the back seat and Justin took the wheel.

The roads were still covered with snow and ice, but Justin managed to get them to the doctor's office safely. After X-raying Sylvia's ankle, Dr. Patterson confirmed Athena's diagnosis. Her left ankle was badly sprained.

Chapter Eight

"You'll have to stay off your ankle for a few days, Sylvia," Athena said, "so you might as well remain here on the ranch. You won't be able to go back to work on Monday."

Sylvia sat propped up in Justin's bed, angry with herself for having such a senseless accident. "I can't inconvenience you that way, Athena. Surely I can manage to get back to Houston tomorrow."

"How would you manage at home all alone?" Justin asked. His eyes sought and held hers. "Or would you be all alone?"

His question annoyed her, but she answered it. "I would be alone, Justin," she said, "but I'm sure I would be able to take care of myself."

"You won't inconvenience anyone by staying here," Athena assured her, patting her hand.

Polly could no longer control her disgust and anger with Sylvia for requiring so much attention from the others, and she expressed her feelings vehemently. "You should have been more careful, Sylvia," she snapped. "Look at all the trouble you've caused. Now you've ruined everybody's weekend and poor Athena will have to take care of you."

Sylvia had promised herself she wouldn't allow Polly to upset her this weekend, but the sulking, petite woman had gone too far. Her insides shook with rage. Like everyone else in the room, the offensive words had rendered her mute.

"That won't be necessary," Justin finally said through tight lips. "I will be at the ranch all week and I'll take care of Sylvia. Everyone is free to go."

"Why don't you call Mrs. Bellows," Copland suggested. "She should be able to make things very comfortable for you."

"Maybe I will," Justin said.

"That would be perfect," Athena agreed. "Now Sylvia, don't worry. Everything is going to work out just fine. And the telephone is right here by your bed," she added. "Please make whatever calls you need to make when you feel up to it."

"We'll let you get some rest now," Justin said, signaling the others to leave. He walked over to the bed and gently caressed Sylvia's face with the back of his hand. "Now it's my turn to nurse you back to health."

She smiled at him and took his hand from her face, though the sensation of his touch lingered. "I'm sorry, Justin," she said. "I don't want to interfere with your work."

"Taking care of you for the next few days will be my pleasure, Lovely Lady," he responded. He kissed her lightly on the lips and left her.

After a few minutes, Sylvia took the telephone from the nightstand and began dialing. She explained her accident to her mother and gave her the telephone number at the ranch in case she needed to reach her. She then called Henrika and left a message with her house-keeper informing her she had purchased the vase and had suffered an accident on the Udall ranch. She would contact her on Monday at the store. Later that evening she would call Bluma.

On Sunday afternoon, Mrs. Bellows arrived, and Polly, Athena and Copland prepard to go back to Dallas. They all went in to say goodbye to Sylvia.

If you follow Dr. Patterson's instructions, Sylvia," Athena said, "by the end of the week your ankle should be much improved."

"Yes, please do, Sylvia," Polly added. "I know you wouldn't want Justin to get behind in his work because of you."

"I promise to follow the doctor's orders to the letter," Sylvia smiled.

"Try to relax and enjoy the week," Copland told her, "and we'll see you on Friday. Shall we go, ladies?" he asked, turning to Athena and Polly.

"Just one more thing," Polly said hesitating. "Please concentrate on your work this week, Justin," she instructed, "and let Sylvia take care of herself. Your art is more important than anything else." She glared at Sylvia and walked away.

Athena and Copland gave Sylvia a warm smile and wave, and followed Polly out of the house.

The next morning was sunny and bright, and the snow had begun to melt. Sylvia showered, treated her foot and dressed. The whole ordeal had proved laborious, so she sat down in the living room to rest for a few minutes before attempting to go to breakfast.

"Hi. Did you rest well?" Justin asked, coming into the room.

"Good morning," Sylvia said cheerfully. "I slept very well last night."

"Good. How is your ankle?"

"Much better, but it's still somewhat painful."

"I see." He walked over to her, dropped to his knees and took her foot in his hands. "The swelling is almost gone," he observed. "Do you have shoes you can wear?"

"I only have my snow boots."

"They won't do," he said, getting to his feet. He went to his bedroom and came back with a pair of his bedroom slippers and some thick socks. "Try these," he said.

"Do you mean you have something to wear on your feet other than cowboy boots?" she kidded, pulling on the socks and sticking her feet into his slippers. "I would have guessed that instead of bedroom slippers you would have bedroom cowboy boots." She looked up at Justin. He was laughing so hard, he was on his knees and gasping for breath. "What's so funny," she asked. He pointed to her feet and she realized his shoes were so big on her she must have looked like a circus clown. She thought about how silly she must look and was prompted to join him in laughter.

When Justin was able to speak again, he asked, "Are you ready for breakfast?"

"I'm starved." He picked her up and carried her in his arms to the breakfast nook. They settled themselves at the table and Mrs. Bellows served them breakfast.

"How will you spend your day?" he asked.

"Reading. I saw a number of books in your library that look interesting."

"I'm glad you've found something to keep you occupied."

"Will you work all day?"

"My day started at five this morning," he told her, "and it probably won't end until late tonight."

"In that case, I guess I won't see you until tomorrow."

"No, no, Sylvia," he said, his sensuous lips forming a smile. "You won't get rid of me that easily. I'll see you at lunch."

After breakfast, Justin carried her back to the living room. He helped her settle herself in a chair by the window and pulled the books she had expressed an interest in from the shelves. "I have something that you may find useful," he said, going to the closet and taking out an exquisitely-carved walking cane. "It belonged to my grandfather."

"Justin," she said, taking the cane from him. "It's beautiful."

"His grandfather carved it and gave it to him when he was a young man. It should help make your life a little easier," he said. With both hands resting on the arms of her chair, he leaned over and kissed her, allowing his lips to linger on hers before his kiss grew deeper and more demanding. "Enjoy your books," he said, pulling away from her. He left for his studio.

Although she tried, it was difficult for Sylvia to concentrate on her book after Justin left. She hobbled about the room on the cane in her big, floppy shoes, turning on the stereo one minute and trying the TV the next. Nothing held her attention but thoughts of Justin. Eventually, she was able to rein her romantic daydreaming and concentrate on her book.

It was one o'clock in the afternoon when Mrs. Bellows brought her a message from Justin. "Mr. Udall would like to know if you'd like to take a short carriage ride."

"I'd love that, Mrs. Bellows."

"Then get dressed," she smiled. "He's waiting for you."

Sylvia pulled on her red slacks and sweater and one snow boot. She took her fur jacket, and made her way to the common living area. Justin was waiting there. He helped her into her jacket and buttoned it from top to bottom. He then carried her outside through the side door.

"Well, what do you think?" he asked.

Sylvia's eyes swept over a steel-gray, four-wheeled vehicle, which was a stunning replica of a carriage from the early 1900's. The convertible top was pulled back, revealing its rich red leather interior. Chancellor was hitched to it and waiting.

"It's beautiful!" Sylvia was impressed.

"I thought you might like it."

With Sylvia still in his arms, Justin started toward the carriage door. "Wait Justin, I haven't spoken to Chancellor." He then walked closer to the horse and she began stroking the animal's nose. "You're a beauty," she whispered. "A real beauty." Chancellor nuzzled her. "He remembers me," she said.

"Of course, he remembers you," Justin said, helping her into the carriage and gently placing her foot on a pillow. "How could he forget such a lovely lady?"

Sylvia was almost giddy as she watched Justin climb into the carriage. "I've never ridden in one of these before," she said. "I feel like Cinderella going to the ball."

Justin laughed. "I think you'll like the ride. Is your foot okay?"

"Yes, it's fine."

He climbed up beside her, linked his arm in hers and took the reins. They rode out over the grassland, through slightly rolling hills, until they reached the edge of a brook where Justin stopped the carriage. A grove of tall Texas pine trees stood to the right.

"That's where my grandfather's first house was built," Justin said, pointing to a spot just beyond the stream. "Only the fireplace and chimney remain."

"Interesting," Sylvia said, surveying the area. I can see why he chose this spot. The view from here is beautiful."

"Yes, it is," Justin agreed.

A large flock of blackbirds flew overhead breaking the stillness of the day.

"What a pretty sight." Sylvia's eyes followed the birds as they lit atop the tall trees.

The air was chilling, and Sylvia took the plaid blanket that was folded next to her and began spreading it over her legs. Justin drew her closer to him and secured the blanket over both of them. He then started the carriage down a path that led to the far end of the ranch. The cold air stung their faces as Chancellor took them deeper into the woods.

"I'm enjoying this, Justin," Sylvia said. "The ride is surprisingly smooth. Did this carriage belong to your grandfather, also?"

"No," Justin answered. "I bought it at an auction in Dallas three years ago."

Sylvia snuggled closer to him and tightened the blanket around her knees. "Is it getting colder?" she asked.

"No, we've turned north and you're feeling the north wind. We'll make another turn soon and it won't seem as cold."

He guided Chancellor around a fallen branch that was blocking the path. The snow in that section of the woods was deep and had not yet begun to melt. For miles and miles, they could see the white, gently rolling hills through the trees.

"I spent many happy days with my grandfather in these woods hunting when I was a boy." Justin's voice softened, and his eyes lit up as he talked about his childhood years with his grandfather.

"Were you a good hunter?"

"Not really," Justin laughed. "I'd go hunting with Grandfather just to be with him and hear the exciting stories he would tell. He taught me a lot."

"Your grandfather must have been a wonderful man."

"I loved him very much."

They rode for another quarter of a mile before Justin stopped the carriage by a giant old oak tree. He slipped his arm around Sylvia's shoulders and she rested her head on his chest. They sat quietly for several minutes before Justin cupped her chin in his fingers and raised her lips to his. Strong feelings of desire gripped Sylvia and she wrapped her arms around Justin's neck and pressed her body longingly against his. Their lips clung together. Justin's probing, demanding kisses ignited a fire inside of her that threatened to consume her very being.

Abruptly, Justin pulled away from her and took the

reins. "I'd better get you back," he whispered in a voice thick with emotion.

When they came out of the woods they were on the east side of the ranch close to the creek. The wind was now behind them and Chancellor's gait had changed.

"We're moving faster," Sylvia said.

"Yes, Chancellor knows he's getting closer to the ranch. After a long run, he's always happy to return home."

Their ride had taken over an hour. When they arrived back at the house, Mrs. Bellows served them lunch. Justin then went back to his studio to work and Sylvia returned to his living quarters.

Her afternoon was spent very much like her morning—reading, TV and music. At half past six, she started to dress for dinner. Mrs. Bellows had told her dinner would be served at seven. She decided to wear a dress she had picked up while shopping on Friday. She had bought it because of its Christmas colors. She thought it would be nice to wear during the holidays. It was a wool jersey, red and green plaid floor-length dress with long sleeves and white satin collar and cuffs. She slipped it over her head, combed her hair, and in Justin's bedroom slippers, joined him in the dining room.

After dinner, they had tea with brandy in Justin's living area, while they listened to music and played a game of backgammon. At eleven o'clock, Justin kissed Sylvia goodnight and went back to his studio.

The days that followed were spent very much like

their first day together—the meals together, rides before lunch, his work and her reading, music and TV.
However, on Thursday after lunch, the routine changed.

"Get your jacket," Justin said. "I want to show you
something."

Sylvia got her coat and followed Justin outside. He
closed the door behind them and escorted her down the
path to his studio. When they walked inside, Sylvia
looked at him in amazement. "What did I do to deserve
this honor?" she asked. She had wanted to ask to see his
work all week, but refused to give him the satisfaction
of turning her down.

Justin smiled at her triumphantly. "You've been a
good little girl," he said. He helped her out of her jacket
and over to a chair which sat in front of a huge covered
canvas. "Close your eyes," he directed her. Sylvia
closed her eyes and could sense him unveiling the
canvas. "Now you may open them," he said.

Sylvia lifted her lashes slowly. After staring at the
canvas for several seconds, her mouth fell open and
tears sprang to her eyes."

"Do you know what it represents?" he asked. Unable
to speak, she nodded her head. "Thank you, Sylvia," he
said hoarsely, "for inspiring me to create the best canvas
I've ever painted in my life."

For a long while she gazed at the canvas and did not
speak. Her mind traveled back to the first evening Justin
had spent with her in Houston. The readings. He had
seemed deeply moved by them at the time, but she
hadn't realized he had been moved to create such a
profound work of art. His interpretations of the various
poems had been linked together on canvas with deep,
earthy oil paints, like a mural painting. Slowly, Sylvia

studied it and chills crawled up her spine as she looked at a scene from The Lynching by Paul McKay. The realness of the pain and agony in the faces on the canvas brought tears to her eyes. The painting further displayed Justin's extraordinary skill as an artist. As she looked at a beautiful black woman in song, a sense of peacefulness surrounded her, edging away the sadness she had felt just a moment earlier. She recognized Malindy from Paul Laurence Dunbar's When Malindy Sings. A broad smile crossed her face when she looked at the last scene on the canvas. It was from Drizzle, one of her favorite poems by Dunbar, and depicted two elderly ladies sitting on a porch talking. One was happily chatting away, while the other wore an expression of boredom.

"It's brilliant, Justin," she finally said, finding it hard to tear her eyes from the painting.

"I'm glad you like it."

"To say I like it would be an understatement. I love it."

He walked over to her and took her hand in his. "I never would have done it if I hadn't heard your ingenious readings of those beautiful poems."

"What will you do with it?" she asked, realizing she would hate to see the painting sold.

"We won't discuss that now."

Hurt by his brushoff, her eyes moved back to the painting. "You're working in oil again."

"For that painting, yes."

"Thank you for showing it to me, Justin," she said, walking over to take one last look at the canvas. "It is really magnificent."

Justin walked behind her and placed his hands on her

shoulders. "So are you, Sylvia," he murmured gently, turning her to face him. He gazed longingly into her eyes for several moments before his mouth claimed hers. His arms dropped to her waist and he pressed her lithe body gently, but firmly against his, as the fervor of his kisses intensified. Spontaneously, Sylvia wrapped her arms around his neck and eagerly returned his passion. His hands began to move artfully over her body. Sylvia felt as if she was caught up in a whirlwind, her desire mounting with each caress. She managed to regain control of herself, and turned her face away from his burning lips. "No, Justin," she whispered breathlessly. He held her for a moment longer, before dropping his arms. "I think we should go now," she said, nervously smoothing her clothing.

He took her hand and led her out of the studio. As they walked back to the house, Sylvia almost felt relieved that the week would soon be over. She didn't know how much longer she could resist her emotions.

On Friday, Sylvia got out of the antique four-poster bed, aware that she had only one more night to sleep in Justin's bed. It had been a wonderful week. Her friendship with Justin had grown, as had her love for him. She was almost thankful for the silly accident. There was still conflict between them concerning his work, but she was hopeful it would soon be resolved. Her ankle was better now, and she no longer had to treat it or wear Justin's big floppy bedroom slippers, or use the lovely cane. Although she wore his thick socks for shoes around the house, she was now able to slip into her snow boots whenever she went outside.

Her day passed very much the same as they all had during the week. However, tonight Athena and Copland would join them for dinner. She had just finished dressing and was looking out the window, when she saw the DeForest's car making its way up the driveway. She hurried to meet them and they all embraced.

"I see you're much better," Copland observed.

"I'm fine," Sylvia smiled.

"I told you it'd only take a week for you to feel better," Athena said.

Justin came in and greeted his sister and brother-in-law. After Athena and Copland had freshened up, they all took their places at the table and Mrs. Bellows served dinner.

"How did things go in Dallas this week," Sylvia asked.

"Oh, the city is back to normal," Athena answered. "The people are busy doing their Christmas shopping and we're doing very well at the gallery."

"We're finishing up exams and getting grades out," Copland added. "This is a pretty busy time at the university."

"Sounds like you've been working very hard," Sylvia said, "while I've done nothing more this week than enjoy myself."

Justin stopped eating for a moment and gazed at her. "You've been a wonderful companion for me." He spoke softly and directly to Sylvia. "My week has been perfect because of you."

The compliment was more than Sylvia expected to hear from Justin. A warm sensation ran up her spine and she smiled at him. "Thank you, Justin," she said.

They were having dessert, when the telephone rang. "It's for you, Mr. Udall," Mrs. Bellows announced. "It's Mr. Newman Willton from New York."

The table fell silent. Hurriedly, Justin got up from his chair and rushed to the telephone. Sylvia thought she detected Copland and Athena exchanging a knowing glance, but she could not imagine what it meant. They attempted to resume their conversation, absently offering each other disjointed sentences. The air was tense with expectation as they impatiently awaited Justin's return. When at last he rejoined them at the table, he wore a pensive expression.

"The showing was a tremendous success," he said nonchalantly. "The critics have given me exceptional reviews."

Copland and Athena were overjoyed with the news and enthusiastically congratulated him.

Sylvia looked at them blankly. "What showing? What critics?" she asked.

"I've had a showing of my work in New York City," Justin informed her, "and it has been acclaimed by several of the city's leading art critics."

"I'm very happy for you, Justin," Sylvia said, sincerely pleased with his achievement. "That's the best news I've heard in a long time. Congratulations."

"Thank you."

"Why didn't you tell me you were showing your work in New York?"

"It didn't concern you, Sylvia," he said matter-of-factly.

"I see." She wondered why Justin's work always somehow managed to come between them. Perhaps some day she would find out.

Justin got up from the table and walked over to the window. "You leave tomorrow." It was a statement more than a question.

"Yes," she replied.

"Good," he said, and left the room.

Athena and Copland looked embarrassed, and attempted to apologize for Justin's strange behavior. Sylvia smiled placidly and assured them she would survive his insult.

The next day Justin drove Sylvia to the airport. Most of the trip was driven in silence. When conversation was attempted, Justin asked Sylvia specific questions to which she gave short, sweet responses.

"I'll call you in a few days," he said, walking her to board her plane.

"Don't bother, Justin," she replied coolly. "I think we both would be better off if you don't."

"I know I've been a little unreasonable, but that's no cause for you to never want to speak to me again."

"It's all the cause I need, Mr. Udall."

Taking her by the shoulders, he turned her to him. "Sylvia, please be patient. I promise I'll explain everything to you later, but you'll have to give me time to work things out in my own way." They stared at each other before he slowly permitted his sensuous lips to meld with hers. "I'll call you in a few days, Miss Random." He released her and walked away.

Back in Houston, Sylvia returned to her routine. She was able to keep herself busy, but was quite unsuccessful in keeping her mind off Justin. She missed him terribly. Now, more than ever, she was acutely aware of how much he meant to her. Henrika had noticed her detachment and had made mention on several occasions that Sylvia seemed to be preoccupied. Yet, she functioned, putting in long hours at the store and taking part in various social activities. Today, had been a particularly long and tiring day. Sylvia was glad to get home.

After a shower and a light dinner of soup and salad, she turned on the TV to the evening news and crawled into bed with a magazine. She was flipping absently through the magazine when the words 'Texas artist' caught her attention. Her eyes went immediately to the TV screen. She recognized Justin's work, and with the remote control she increased the volume. The reporter was extolling the talents of a Texas artist who was thrilling the New York art world with his paintings of Texas scenery and culture—Justin Udall. He reported that Mr. Udall's New York showing had been such a success, he had been invited to exhibit in London, and was at that moment in flight to that city.

Sylvia's heart sank as she realized Justin had chosen not to share his moment of triumph with her.

Chapter Nine

The store had been busy all day. Now, the last two hours before closing, it was practically empty. It was Christmas Eve and most people had finished their holiday shopping. There were a few stragglers about, and Sylvia watched them disinterestedly. She and Mary were the only two salespeople in the Nook of International Treasures. She stood against a far wall, reviewing her plans for Christmas Day. She was scheduled to have afternoon dinner with her parents and family in Clear Lake City, after which she would drive back to Houston to a cocktail party at Henrika's mansion in River Oaks. She would then go to Bluma's for a second Christmas dinner with friends.

Finally, the bell rang signaling the closing of the store. Sylvia and Mary closed out and left Emary Oaks. What a day, Sylvia thought to herself, as she walked through the shopping mall. She studied the faces of the last-minute shoppers she passed with interest and wondered about their lives. What made some faces happy and alive, others sad, some depressed and lonely, while others simply looked blank. She chuckled to herself and wondered about the message emanating from her face.

Sylvia got into her car and headed for home. As she drove, her week on the ranch with Justin flashed in her mind. She smiled as she thought of how right she had felt in his four-poster bed and silk pajamas. She could still see him on his knees laughing at her when she had first slipped into his thick socks and bedroom slippers. Justin carrying her to and from meals in his arms, even after she was able to walk on her own, would always be a treasured memory. Long after she had returned to Houston, Sylvia had questioned whether or not the long carriage rides they had taken together was a figment of her imagination. But she knew his strong arm linked with hers, the heat from his body warming her and the sweet smell of him had all been very real. Unimagined also were the quiet evenings they had shared in his quarters playing backgammon, listening to music and talking. Then the images of that special Thursday deluged her thoughts—his studio, the magnificent painting, his touch that had aroused such passion in her. It had been a wonderful week and she would always treasure the memory of it.

She parked her car and forced her mind to focus on the present. Gifts had to be wrapped before she went to Bluma's second annual Christmas tree decorating party, and she dreaded the thought of wrapping them alone. Once inside her condo, she reluctantly made her way to the closet and took out paper, ribbons and boxes. Last year she and Armand had spent Christmas Eve wrapping their gifts together and had made a happy champagne party out of the occasion. But now the gift wrapping was just a task that had to be done. She put some holiday music on the stereo, and with great speed and precision, but no creativity or joy, finished the gifts within the hour. She checked her packages against her gift list, saw that she had omitted no one, and packed them in a large tote bag to be distributed on Christmas Day. Then she dressed for Bluma's party.

Sylvia did not want to evoke further memories of Justin, so she decided not to wear the long green and red plaid dress she had bought for holiday occasions. Instead she wore navy wool slacks and a white silk shirt, and pulled on a pair of highly-polished navy blue leather boots. She slipped into her fur jacket and went to the party.

Bluma's small townhouse was crowded with mutual friends. They sat on the floor, sofa and chairs, laughing and talking. When Sylvia entered, everyone cheered.

"You're late," Bluma greeted her. "We've been waiting for you so we can begin decorating the tree."

"Sorry," Sylvia apologized.

"We'll forgive you this time, Sylvia," Perry, Bluma's fiance, teased her. "Just don't let it happen again next year."

"I won't," she promised, following the group over to the six-foot evergreen.

The fragrance of the tree had permeated the room, giving it the sweet smell of Christmas. Bluma wanted an old-fashioned Christmas tree, so baked gingerbread men, strung popcorn and nuts were to be used for decorations. The group began hanging the ornaments, all the while laughing and teasing each other. Sylvia joined in their merriment, absently hanging little gingerbread men everywhere she could reach and somehow laughing on cue. But her heart and mind were elsewhere. She thought of Justin and Polly and wondered if the petite young woman had accompanied him to London. Gradually her thoughts moved to Armand. She missed him.

They finished the tree and Bluma led the group in singing several holiday songs, before serving them a supper of homemade soup, bread, salad and hot apple cider. The mood was now subdued as they sat around chatting.

Sylvia went to the kitchen and began washing dishes. She gave her thoughts free rein, deciding she might as well had worn the long green and red plaid dress since her mind insisted on focusing on Justin Udall.

"What are you doing in here?" Bluma interrupted her.

Bluma's sudden intrusion startled her. "I'm doing the dishes," she snapped.

"You're supposed to be out there enjoying yourself, Sylvia."

"Bluma, I'm the only one out there who is alone. I feel out of place."

"How can you feel alone when there are over a dozen people in that room who love you?"

Sylvia eyed her friend somberly. "You know what I mean," she said.

"Yes, I know," Bluma conceded, perching on a stool in the small kitchen. "Be patient, Sylvia," she said sympathetically. "Things will work out."

"Promises, promises," Sylvia smiled stiffly, putting away the last of the dishes. She glanced at her friend who was gazing at her with great concern. "I'm all right, Bluma," she said. "Really I am."

"Didn't he promise to call," Bluma asked.

"Yes," Sylvia answered, walking to the kitchen door, "but I doubt if I'll hear from Justin. And even if he does call, I'm not sure I want to talk with him. I'm tired of the merry-go-round, Bluma."

"Don't make any rash decisions," Bluma advised her. "You're just a little blue because it's the holiday season. You'll feel better after the new year arrives."

Sylvia laughed. "That's a whole week from now," she said. "That's a long time to have to wait to feel better." She left the kitchen to rejoin the others, with her friend close behind.

Christmas morning was sunny and cold. Sylvia, with her tote bag filled with gifts, drove to Clear Lake City to celebrate Christmas Day with her parents and other relatives. She loved family gatherings and looked forward to seeing everyone, though she expected to be bombarded with questions. She knew her Aunt Bea and cousins Lotona and Jasmine had been terribly disappointed over her broken engagement to Armand. Aunt Bea prided herself on predicting births and marriages for family members, and never once had she been wrong. She had predicted Sylvia would marry early the following year, but now those plans had been changed. Sylvia hoped her aunt would not take her broken engagement too hard.

When she arrived at her parents' home, she could tell by the cars that everyone was there. She hoped she was not late. She grabbed her tote bag and went inside.

"I've been waiting for you," her Aunt Bea said, embracing her. She held Sylvia at arms length, gazing at her as if she expected to see something out of the ordinary. "You look terrific," she finally said.

"Thanks, Aunt Bea," Sylvia replied. "So do you." She greeted her parents, grandparents, uncles and cousins, and then added her gifts to the pile of presents already under the tree.

"Now, Sylvia," her aunt said, taking her aside and speaking confidentially. "Is your marriage to Armand definitely cancelled?"

"Yes, Aunt Bea, it's definitely cancelled."

Sylvia's mother joined them in the far corner of the living room where her aunt had solicitiously escorted her. "What are you two whispering about?" she asked.

"I'm trying to find out from Sylvia if there's the slightest possibility she may change her mind about marrying that nice young man, Armand."

"Sylvia's mother looked at her sympathetically. "I think she has made up her mind, Bea," she said.

"But why, Sylvia?" her aunt persisted. She was thoughtful for a moment and then with a glimmer of hope asked, "Have you found someone else?"

Sylvia squirmed in her seat and tried to avoid their eyes. She was not in the mood to discuss Justin, but realized she had never been able to lie successfully to her mother or her aunt. "W...W...Well, not really," she stammered.

Both older women looked shocked. "You never told me there was another man involved," her mother said.

"No other man is involved," Sylvia informed them. "I realized I don't love Armand and broke our engagement."

"You're not seeing another young man?" her aunt asked, attempting to get a clear understanding once and for all.

Sylvia sighed deeply and looked from one to the other.

"There is someone else," her mother said with a note of finality.

"Yes," Sylvia nodded.

"Then there will be a wedding after all," her aunt said happily.

"No," Sylvia shook her head.

"Now, darling," her mother said, taking her daughter's hands in hers, "what seems to be the problem?"

Sylvia decided to end the conversation at that moment, so she told them the truth. "I love him but he doesn't love me."

Her aunt looked amused. "Did he tell you he doesn't love you?" she asked.

"No," Sylvia confessed.

"Then let's not rule out the possibility of a wedding," she said. "I'm sure it's just a matter of time before he asks you to be his wife. You're a very special kind of woman, Sylvia."

"Don't count on it, Aunt Bea," Sylvia said, getting to her feet. "I'll help you get dinner on the table, Mother."

"There's one other little thing," her Aunt Bea said slowly. "I brought the dress for you to try on."

"What dress?" Sylvia questioned.

"My wedding gown," she answered matter-of-factly. "There's a possibility alterations may be needed. If so, we'll want to get all of that done early."

Sylvia shook her head hopelessly, as they went to the kitchen and began putting Christmas dinner on the table.

"Are you going to tell us anything about this young man you're in love with, Sylvia?" her mother asked hesitantly.

"I don't want to talk about him, Mother," she replied.

"I'm sure he's just as nice as Armand," Bea assured her sister. "Sylvia, I'm just thrilled you're going to be

married in my gown. None of the other girls in the
family, of course, is tall enough to wear it. Now
promise me," she went on, "you'll pass it on to your
daughter. I hope she grows to be six-feet tall like you
and me," she finished thoughtfully.

Sylvia wondered if her aunt had heard a word she had
said. Not only had she married her off in her wedding
gown to a man who had shown no interest in making her
his wife, but she had also given her a six-foot tall
daughter. She had to stifle a smile, realizing the
probability of having a child that tall if she and Justin
were to marry.

"There's no reason to rush things, Aunt Bea. You
may have a very long wait before you see me march
down the aisle in your gown."

"I just have a feeling, Sylvia," she said. "I have a
feeling to get things done now."

The family seated themselves around the dining room
table and shared the lovely Christmas dinner Sylvia's
mother had prepared. She was thankful that during
dinner Aunt Bea's attention was diverted to various
other members of the family. They finished dinner and
cleaned the kitchen. Afterwards, they all opened their
gifts.

A couple of hours passed and Sylvia began gathering
her belongings to make her way back to Houston and
Sylvia's cocktail party.

"Come," Bea said, when she noticed that Sylvia was
preparing to leave. "You'll have to try the dress on. It'll
only take a few minutes."

Sylvia followed her aunt, her mother and her two
cousins into the bedroom. Aunt Bea took her wedding
gown from the garment bag and held it in front of her.

It looked more beautiful to Sylvia now than it had when her Aunt Bea first realized the young girl could wear it and showed it to her when she was seventeen years old. The empire waist style gown was made of ivory lace, and had many tiny buttons down the back and on the long sleeves. When Sylvia slipped into the dress, gasps escaped the lips of everyone in the room. It fit perfectly and she looked beautiful. She glanced at herself in the mirror, admiring how the skirt hung straight and loose from the high waistline.

"If I should ever marry, Aunt Bea," she said, "I would be honored to wear this dress."

"You look like a dream," her mother said, embracing her.

"I'm so glad you like it," Bea said tearfully.

Sylvia left her mother's house determined not to think about the dress or marrying anyone—especially Justin Udall. Thoughts of that kind would only lead to sadness and heartache.

She pulled in front of Henrika's house in River Oaks and gave her keys to the valet to park her car. She was led into the ballroom where close to two hundred people were gathered. Sylvia moved about slowly, smiling at everyone she passed as she looked for Henrika. She finally spotted her across the room and they waved at each other. While her hand was still in mid air, a man grasped her fingers and pressed them to his lips.

"You're very beautiful," the man said, and attempted to draw her into his arms.

Sylvia stiffened, and with diplomacy pulled away from him. "Thank you," she smiled sweetly, and moved further into the crowd. She didn't get very far before a tall, stately, silver-haired woman stopped her.

"Aren't you the buyer for the Nook of International Treasures?" she asked.

"Yes," Sylvia answered.

The woman moved closer to her and spoke in whispered tones. "When will you get more paintings by that Udall man?" she asked. "I've got to have something of his and Henrika says you're the only person who could possibly get him to sell to Emary Oaks."

"We will probably never carry Mr. Udall's works again," Sylvia informed her.

"But dear, you don't understand," the woman continued. "My friend has a Udall and I just simply must have one."

"Then I suggest you go to his studio in Dallas," Sylvia said. "I'll be happy to give you the address."

The woman stepped back from Sylvia as if she had hit her and for a moment appeared to be in shock. "My dear, I have never been to Dallas in my life and I certainly have no plans of ever going. Not even for a Udall." She eyed Sylvia with disgust and walked away.

The evening advanced rapidly. Sylvia moved about chatting with several of the guests. Before long, it was time to leave for Bluma's. She said her goodbyes and left the party.

By the time Sylvia arrived at Bluma's for her second Christmas dinner of the day, she was exhausted. It did not disturb her that she was alone and Bluma and Perry and the other two couples appeared to be happy and very much in love. Her only concern was spending an appropriate amount of time with her friends, eating as little as possible, and getting home so that she could get some rest. She cleverly managed to leave right after dinner. By ten o'clock, she was home and in bed. She drifted off to sleep effortlessly, and slept through the night.

It was seven forty-five when the telephone rang, jolting her out of a deep sleep. From under her covers, Sylvia counted the rings as she wondered who her caller could be. Perhaps it was Aunt Bea calling to share more of her plans for Sylvia's nonexistent wedding. On the twelfth ring, she lifted the receiver and spoke into it huskily.

"Good morning, Lovely Lady." Sharp sensations gripped her heart and for a moment she was unable to speak.

"What do you want, Justin?" she asked coldly when she found her voice again.

Taken aback by her tone, his mood changed. "I'd like to talk with you, Sylvia," he said evenly.

Intense anger welled up in her. How dare he wait until the morning after Christmas to call her. Memories flooded back of how coolly he had dismissed her when she had inquired about his work in Dallas. She recalled how he had gone off to London without a word, and the humiliation she felt when she had to learn of his success from a TV screen. Who knew what other stunts he would pull. Totally irritated, she hung up the phone and snuggled down under her covers.

Again the ringing telephone punctuated the silence of her room. When she finally decided to answer it on the eighth ring, she was shaken by the venom in Justin's voice.

"Don't you ever do that again," he growled, emphasizing each word. "I'll see you in twenty minutes. Goodbye." He hung up the phone and Sylvia jumped out of bed.

By the time she had taken a quick shower, combed her hair and pulled on a pair of jeans and a sweater, Justin was ringing her doorbell.

"Good morning, Sylvia," he said brusquely, and stepped inside the door. "Get your coat, we're going to breakfast."

Her temper flared. "Who do you think you are, Justin, coming in here and ordering me around?"

"I know who I am, lady." His voice was low and somber. "Now, get your coat."

She gazed at him and saw the serious look in his eyes. She slipped into her jacket and followed him out to a rented car. Silently they drove to the Warwick Hotel, went to the dining room and ordered breakfast.

"Are you going to tell me what this is all about?" Sylvia finally asked.

"Where's Armand?" he demanded.

"Justin, you sound like a broken record," she said. "If you are so interested in Armand, why didn't you drag him out of his bed this morning to have breakfast with you?"

"I'm not in the mood to repeat myself, Sylvia," he stated tersely.

"I don't know where Armand is," she said with exasperation. We're no longer friends." She thought she noticed a flicker of satisfaction cross his face, but his mood was not visibly altered.

"Who did you spend Christmas with? You were out all day."

"My family, Sylvia and Bluma," she replied, realizing he had tried to get her while she was out.

"I see." They finished breakfast, he paid the bill and ushered her out of the hotel. "Let's take a walk," he said. Remembering the last walk she had taken with Armand, she hesitated. "What's the problem," he asked.

"Nothing, really I guess. It's just that the last walk I took with someone turned out to be a disaster."

He eyed her curiously. "Let's hope this one turns out differently."

Fearing Justin might suggest Bell Park for their walk since it was close by, Sylvia hurriedly suggested they walk through the zoo. Justin was amused by the idea, and drove the short distance to Hermann Park.

For a long while, they walked along looking at the animals and talking casually. Sylvia wondered how long it would take Justin to tell her why he had come to see her. They walked until they came to an isolated bench under a tree and sat down. The wind was cold and they sat close together.

"Since I saw you last, I've spent most of my time between New York and London," Justin said. "My career has finally taken the turn that I hoped for. I've been accepted as a major American artist. I'll be showing my work not only in several cities in this country, but also some major European cities."

"I know, Justin. I learned all about your promising career from the six o'clock news and the papers." Her tone was very sarcastic.

"I realize you must think I've been unreasonable concerning you and my work," he said, "but it was important to me to direct my own career. The very last thing I wanted to happen was for a very beautiful and very capable young woman by the name of Sylvia Random to make me a star." For the first time that day, Justin smiled. "It was imperative," he said looking at her closely, "that I handle things my way."

"You have quite an ego, Justin."

"No, Sylvia," he said, shaking his head. "Not ego, but faith and determination that the plan and timetable I made for myself would be successful."

"Now what?" she asked, getting up from the bench and turning her coat collar up to warm her neck. Justin got to his feet and slipped his arm around her waist. They began to walk again.

"Now I'm ready to negotiate an agreement with Emary Oaks to have exclusive rights to sell my work in Houston."

His words stopped her dead in her tracks. "Are you teasing me, Justin?" she asked seriously.

"I wouldn't do that, Sylvia. I'm quite serious."

"Then the early morning wake-up call was worth it," she said.

Justin didn't respond. They continued to walk and look at the animals. Finally he guided her back to the car and drove her home.

"Would you like some coffee?" she asked as he stood inside her door.

"No," he answered. "I haven't slept in twenty-four hours. I'm going back to the hotel to get some rest. Have dinner with me tonight, Sylvia."

Her eyes searched his face before she answered. She had never seen him look so tired and worn out before. "I'd like that," she said. He left, promising to pick her up at seven.

Sylvia sank into a chair and closed her eyes. At last the pieces had fallen into place. It was a relief to finally understand why Justin had never wanted her to handle his work. He was determined to direct his own career. From the very beginning he had resented her buying his art for Emary Oaks and her attempts at controlling his work in Houston. Now that he had gained his success according to his plan and timing, he was handing her what she wanted—exclusive rights to his work in Houston—on a silver platter. She smiled when she thought of telling Henrika the news. Maybe now, the stately lady at the Christmas party could at last own a Udall.

But would this alone end their merry-go-round relationship? He had questioned her thoroughly about her relationship with Armand, but what about his relationship with Polly? She had been foolish not to ask him about it. She sighed softly and shifted in her chair. By the time I crawl into bed tonight, she thought, me and Justin will probably have found some reason to be angry with each other. The proverbial ending to their perfect times together. She went through the day in a semi-daze.

Readying herself for her dinner date with Justin, Sylvia stepped out of the tub and dried herself briskly with a large bath towel. She rubbed a rich lavender cream into her skin, giving her perfect copper complexion a healthy glow. She pulled on a salmon-colored, long-sleeved wool knit dress with a deep-scooped neckline and a softly gathered skirt. With it, she wore chocolate leather pumps and her diamond stud earrings. Impatiently, she waited for Justin to arrive.

When she opened the door ten minutes later and looked at him, her heart began to pound. He looked well-rested and extremely handsome in his dark gray pin-striped suit, blue shirt, navy and burgundy tie and, of course, the cowboy boots. How could she have ever thought that all she wanted from Justin Udall was a signed agreement stating he would sell his work only to Emary Oaks. Looking at him now, she knew what she had told her mother and her Aunt Bea at Christmas was indeed fact. She loved him and wanted much, much more from Justin than she felt he was willing to give.

"Hi," he said, coming into the room carrying a large package. He kissed her lightly on the nose.

"Hi," she responded.

He propped the package against the sofa and smiled at her. "A belated Christmas gift," he said. "Merry Christmas."

Surprised, she stared at the package before returning her gaze to him. "I'm very embarrassed, Justin," she said. "I don't have a gift for you."

Slowly his eyes caressed her face. "You have a gift for me, Sylvia," he assured her softly. She looked at him questioningly. "You can give it to me later."

Her thoughts moved about in a hundred different directions, but she refused to focus on any specific one. In her heart she knew whatever she had that Justin wanted from her this night, he would have it, with all of her love.

"Go ahead and open it," he encouraged her.

With trembling fingers, she tore the paper from the package and another shock wave hit her. Slowly her eyes met his. "You can't give this away," she said.

"Of course, I can," he smiled.

Her eyes moved slowly from Justin to the magnificent painting inspired by her readings of poetry, and then back to him. "Justin, this canvas is invaluable."

"So is our friendship," he said.

Not able to believe that Justin was actually giving her his masterpiece, she continued her argument. "But don't you want to show this with your other work?" she asked.

"Maybe you'll lend it to us sometimes."

She looked at the painting for a long time. "Maybe sometimes I won't," she said, feeling that once she fully accepted the gift from Justin she would be too selfish to share it with anyone else. "I'm not sure I should accept this painting, Justin," she persisted. "It's much too valuable."

He went to her and took her face in his hands. "It's yours, Sylvia," he said. "I painted it expressly for you." He lowered his face to hers and kissed her tenderly, but deeply. "We'd better go to dinner now," he said hoarsely.

Sylvia ate very little at dinner. Justin's promised business agreement with Emary Oaks and the splendid painting he had given her as a Christmas gift had her completely overwhelmed. All the way back to her condo, she wondered what she should do about the painting.

"Would you like coffee or tea?" she asked, as she opened the door and lead the way into the living room.

"No, thank you." His mood was serious. "But I would like my Christmas gift now." Sylvia's breath caught in her throat and her eyes fixed on the painting he had given her. "Sylvia." He spoke her name softly and reached out for her.

Thoughts raced through Sylvia's mind, for she knew

what he would ask for and she knew what her answer would be. Tonight she would give him the Christmas gift he wanted. In some dark corner of her mind, she wondered if she would regret this night. She should have asked him about Polly, but she was afraid. She did not want to hear Justin say he loved the pretty, petite woman. But she also knew that no matter what happened, her love for him would sustain her.

"Sylvia," he whispered her name again, and this time she rushed to him. Justin's arms clamped around her, making her his prisoner. Their moist mouths meshed hungrily. His hands roamed over her back and neck, sending torrid flames of desire racing throughout her being. All the while, he pressed her harder and harder against him. "Sylvia, Sylvia," he whispered each time he tore his lips from hers, and again their mouths would fuse.

Finally, painfully and slowly, he pushed away her sagging body, weak with desire for him, and gazed at her tenderly. "Sylvia, I love you. Will you marry me, Lovely Lady?" he asked softly.

Tears filled Sylvia's eyes as Justin said the words she had waited so long to hear. For the third time that day, Justin had shocked her. But the third shock was the charm. "Oh, Justin, yes," she said, "yes, I'll marry you," and again he held her tightly in his arms.

"I'll be very busy for the next few months," he said when he finally released her. "Do you want to plan the wedding for the spring of next year?" He walked to the door and she followed him. Caressing her face with his fingertips, he spoke to her seriously. "I have never received nor do I ever expect to receive a Christmas gift as precious as the one you've just given me, Sylvia.

Talk to you later, Lovely Lady," he said, as he kissed her lightly on the lips, opened the door and disappeared down the hall.

Sylvia crawled into bed that night thinking of how wrong her prediction had been. The evening had ended with her happier than she had ever been in her life.

Chapter Ten

The next day Sylvia returned to work with that special glow which announced she was a happy woman in love. She sat at her desk humming softly to herself and thumbing through some papers. Henrika walked into the office, plopped in a chair and put her feet up on the desk.

"Are we having very many returns or exchanges?" Sylvia asked.

"No," Henrika answered, "just a small stampede for the sale merchandise."

Sylvia laughed softly and continued to hum a little tune.

"What are you so happy about?" Henrika asked, looking her over closely. Sylvia turned to answer and Henrika threw up a hand to silence her. Mischievously, she pointed a finger at Sylvia. "You've seen Justin," she said.

"How did you know?" Sylvia asked, surprised.

"It's written all over you." Henrika walked over to Sylvia's desk and leaned against it, peering down at the young woman. "You look as if something very special has happened in your life," she said.

"It has, Henrika," she replied, "and you're going to just love part of it. Justin has agreed to give Emary Oaks exclusive rights to his work in Houston."

Henrika gasped and her eyes opened wide in amazement. "You did it!" she exclaimed. "I always knew you would." Her eyes lingered on the young woman. "What else?" she asked. "I can tell there's more you should be telling me."

"Well, Henrika," Sylvia said, attempting to be nonchalant, "Justin asked me to marry him."

Henrika let out a yelp and embraced her. "Have you set the date?"

"The spring," Sylvia answered, beaming.

"That's wonderful."

Sylvia floated through the day in a state of euphoria, and then left to meet Bluma, who had agreed earlier to have coffee with her after work.

"You sounded so happy over the phone, Sylvia, amd you look so radiant," Bluma said, as they sat in a small restaurant sipping steaming mugs of the rich beverage. "What happened?"

"I don't have to wait until after the new year to feel better," Sylvia laughed. "Last night Justin asked me to marry him."

"Sylvia! That's terrific! When?"

"The spring."

Bluma jumped up and leaned over to hug her. "Oh, Sylvia, we'll be marrying at about the same time!"

"I know, Bluma. I'm so happy."

That night Sylvia expected to hear from Justin, but he never called. Anticipating a call from him at work the following day, she stayed close to the office. But again, she was disappointed. By the third day after Sylvia had accepted Justin's proposal of marriage, she still had not heard from him and she was beginning to doubt her own mind. Was Justin's proposal a figment of her imagination or just a cruel joke he had orchestrated to amuse himself? She really should have asked him about his relationship with Polly.

The next day was impossible for Sylvia. Each time the phone rang she hoped it was Justin. Her nerves were frayed and she snapped at everyone in the office. Several times she lifted the receiver from the cradle to telephone Athena, but never followed through. After all, what would she say to her? Your brother asked me to marry him and now has disappeared into thin air? Be patient, Sylvia, she told herself.

She left the store, grateful Bluma had agreed to see a movie with her. A comedy was just what she needed to distract her from thoughts of Justin. She laughed a lot and left the theater feeling a bit more relaxed.

"Feeling better?" Bluma inquired.

"Yes, Bluma, thanks." They pressed through the crowd to the parking lot. "It's just that I miss Justin so very much."

"I understand," Bluma smiled compassionately.

Sylvia went straight to bed when she got home, but couldn't sleep. She tossed and turned most of the night. Finally she decided she would try to read and maybe that would settle her thoughts. It was three a.m. when the telephone rang.

"Why aren't you asleep?" Justin asked when Sylvia answered the phone sounding as if she were wide awake.

"Are you in Houston?" she asked, feeling a surge of joy beginning to flow through her body.

"No, and you didn't answer my question."

"I'm not sleepy. I was reading. Where are you?"

"New York."

"I've been worried about you Justin. Why haven't you called?" The happiness she had first felt when she thought he was close to her was supplemented by a feeling of well-being.

"I'm sorry I worried you," he said, "but I've had a very busy schedule since I last saw you. I've just come in from London where we're planning an exhibit. I feel guilty for calling you at this hour, but I just had to hear your voice."

"I'm happy you called," she whispered. She didn't want to upset him—he sounded so very, very weary. But she had to know. "Justin, where is Polly?"

"I have no idea," he sighed deeply. "Why?"

"Your relationship with her has been bothering me."

"It shouldn't, Sylvia." He sounded confused. "Polly and I are friends. There's nothing more between us."

"She's in love with you," Sylvia persisted.

"Maybe. But I'm in love with you, Lovely Lady," he assured her. "I've missed you so much these last few days."

"I've missed you, too," she said softly. "When will I see you?"

"I'm not sure, honey. Maybe the middle of next month. My schedule is pretty tight."

"I can't wait that long before seeing you, Justin." She could no longer control the frustration she felt. "Surely you can get away before then."

Several seconds elapsed. "Maybe I can get away late New Year's Eve," he said. "But I'll have to leave New Year's Day."

"Great," her tone changed. "We can be married then."

"We can be married when?"

"Late New Year's Eve. I'll make all the arrangements."

"You've got a date," he laughed. "You're crazy, Lovely Lady, and I love you so very, very much."

"I love you too."

Sylvia sat alone at a table in a little coffee shop in the Galleria sipping a cup of tea. It was the only place of its kind open at that time of morning. The coffee shop was crowded with people having breakfast and waiting for orders to take to work with them to eat at their desks. She was busy mentally planning her wedding. Her thoughts were interrupted when Henrika and Bluma joined her at the table.

"Where did you two come from?" she asked, surprised to see her friends.

"We ran into each other in the mall and decided to have coffee before going in to work," Bluma said.

"How is the tea?"

"Good," Sylvia replied, "and I have more news." Her friends ordered coffee and muffins and then turned their attention to her. "I spoke to Justin last night and we're going to be married New Year's Eve," she announced.

"Sylvia," Bluma said excitedly, "that's tomorrow."

"I know. I'm trying to get everything worked out now."

Henrika and Bluma exchanged worried glances. "What needs to be done?" Henrika asked. "Do you need any help?"

"Everything needs to be done," Sylvia said, "and yes, I need all the help I can get."

"Sylvia, this is absurd." Bluma stirred her coffee vigorously. "Have you lost your mind?"

"Don't be upset, Bluma," Henrika said calmly. "It's good to be impulsive once in a while. It's good for the soul and it makes life more interesting." She took a paper napkin from the holder and a pen from her purse. "Now, Sylvia," she said, "let's plan the wedding."

Bluma sighed and rolled her eyes to the ceiling. "Where is all of this taking place? What about the blood tests and the marriage license?"

For a moment Sylvia looked perplexed, but again Henrika came to the rescue. "You will be married in my ballroom and I can get all the legal details taken care of. I know judges, lawyers, doctors and everyone else we'll need to contact. I'll have all the cages of doves at the store moved to my house and get lots and lots of flowers. Oh, this is so much fun," she said, taking another napkin from the holder.

They had completed the details for the wedding and had begun a discussion of the reception, when Henrika covered her mouth with her hand and gazed at them.

"Is something wrong?" Bluma asked, now excited about the wedding plans.

"I forgot I've invited two hundred and fifty people to a New Year's Eve party at my home."

"That's wonderful." Bluma's new-found enthusiasm did not waver. "They will all be guests at the wedding."

Looking as though she should have thought of that idea herself, Henrika began folding her notes and putting them into her purse. "Right. Now we'd better start

getting some of these things done. You know," she
laughed, "we're probably starting a new trend. Next
year all my friends will be having a wedding at their
New Year's Eve parties.

*　*　*

Twenty large white enamel cages, each containing a
pair of doves, were arranged against the walls of the
huge ballroom. One cage sat in the middle of the floor.
Planters holding dozens of brilliant, scarlet long-
stemmed roses sat between the cages. Large deep
green, velvet bows hung on the walls above each
planter. On the stage, which was slightly raised from
the floor, were candlestands with white candles and
more roses arranged with full, lush green house plants.
Although the dance band, which Henrika had engaged
to entertain at her New Year's Eve party, had been set
up on the stage, the area looked like a lovely garden.

At 11:45 p.m., Henrika went to the stage, which
would serve as the altar, and silenced the dance band.
With the microphone in her bejeweled hand, she announced the wedding. Her guests were surprised by this
new twist Henrika had added to her party this year, and
cleared the dance floor so that she could proceed.
Several members of her household staff quickly placed
a white runner down the middle of the floor and bordered it with several candlestands containing white
candles.

With the band softly playing, Sylvia, on her father's
arm and looking more beautiful than she had ever
looked in her life, marched down the white path that had
been laid for her. Gasps escaped the lips of almost

everyone in the room. Some guests could not help but whisper about her beauty. She wore her aunt's ivory lace wedding gown and her hair was in soft curls about her shoulders. On her head was a circlet of tiny white rosebuds entwined with baby's breath. Perfect tiny pearls were in her ears and around her neck. She carried a bouquet of white roses and gardenias, accented with fresh greenery and a spray of baby's breath.

Justin, in formal attire and the black rattlesnake cowboy boots, waited for her at the altar.

The vows were quickly exchanged.

The clock began to strike the midnight hour and everyone joined in the countdown. At midnight, the band started to play a light and airy waltz and Justin led Sylvia out to the middle of the dance floor. Gracefully, they circled the room, both wearing broad smiles as they gazed into each other's eyes.

"I love you," he whispered.

"I love you," she whispered in return. "And I can't think of anything I'd rather be doing than dancing with you at midnight."

Justin pretended to think seriously. "I can think of one thing I'd rather be doing with you right now," he teased, "but I guess I'll just have to wait."

She laughed softly in his ear. "But not long, my love," she boldly assured him.

The music stopped and everyone cheered. Henrika then led her guests in singing Auld Lang Syne. Once more the champagne began to flow, the dance band struck up a currently popular song and the New Year's Eve party gathered momentum.

Justin and Sylvia slipped away from the party and headed for the Warwick Hotel.

"It was a lovely wedding, Sylvia," he said softly, "and you are the most beautiful bride in the world.

She gazed at him lovingly. "And the happiest," she said.

They spent the remainder of the night wishing each other a very Happy New Year.

About the Author

Barbara Stephens is a Harvard University M.A.T. and a former college instructor. She has lived and travelled throughout Europe and the Caribbean. She now makes her home in Houston, Texas. Ms. Stephens is the author of two other romance novels, Wayward Lover and A Toast to Love.